PRAYERS OF AN ACCIDENTAL NATURE

Prayers of an Accidental Nature

STORIES

Debra Di Blasi

COFFEE HOUSE PRESS :: MINNEAPOLIS

COPYRIGHT © 1998 by Debra Di Blasi
COVER ILLUSTRATION by Jenny Hahn
COVER DESIGN by Kelly N. Kofron
AUTHOR PHOTOGRAPH by Laura Bogue

Coffee House Press is supported in part by a grant provided by the Minnesota State Arts Board, through an appropriation by the Minnesota State Legislature, and in part by a grant from the National Endowment for the Arts. Significant support has also been provided by the McKnight Foundation; the Lila Wallace Reader's Digest Fund; Lannan Foundation; Target Stores, Dayton's, and Mervyn's by the Dayton Hudson Foundation; General Mills Foundation; St. Paul Companies; Butler Family Foundation; Honeywell Foundation; Star Tribune Foundation; James R. Thorpe Foundation; Jerome Foundation; the law firm of Schwegman, Lundberg, Woessner & Kluth, P.A.; and many individual donors. To you and our many readers across the country, we send our thanks for your continuing support.

Coffee House Press books are available to the trade through our primary distributor, Consortium Book Sales & Distribution, 1045 Westgate Drive, Saint Paul, MN 55114. For personal orders, catalogs, or other information, write to Coffee House Press, 27 North Fourth Street, Suite 400, Minneapolis, MN 55401.

LIBRARY OF CONGRESS CIP INFORMATION
Di Blasi, Debra, 1957 –
    Prayers of an accidental nature: stories / by Debra Di Blasi.
       p.   cm.
       Contents: The season's condition—Drowning hard—An interview with my husband—Blind—I am telling you lies—Fog—An obscure geography—Where all things converge—Our perversions—Chairman of the board—Pavlov's smile—Prayers of an accidental nature.
    ISBN 1-56889-083-7 (pb: alk paper)
       1. United States—Social life and customs—20th century—Fiction.
I. Title.
PS3554.I1735P73   1999
813'.54—dc21   98-56287
                                                                       CIP

10   9   8   7   6   5   4   3   2   1
first printing / first edition
printed in Canada

CONTENTS

ACKNOWLEDGMENTS The author gratefully acknowledges the following publications in which these stories previously appeared: *Cottonwood,* "Drowning Hard"; *Lovers: Writings by Women* (The Crossing Press) and *New Delta Review,* which awarded the story the Eyster Prize for Fiction, "An Interview with My Husband"; *Colorado-North Review,* "The Season's Condition"; *Sou'wester Review,* "I Am Telling You Lies"; *Transfer,* "Where All Things Converge"; and *TIWA (Themes Interpreted by Writers and Artists),* "Chairman of the Board."

For my mother, Donna Pickens,
and my father, D.E. Pickens,
with love and gratitude

The Season's Condition

THIS WILL BE A SHORT STORY. I have, more or less, promised Glenna that. Glenna is my beautiful, inane sister. She says I ramble when I speak, write, or think. But what does she know? Not much. She does not know, for example, that birds sing at night. They do. I've heard them: chirping in the dark like old women who tell themselves secrets, old sins they don't regret.

Since I moved in with Glenna one month ago, I no longer sleep at night. Not the sleep that shifts you beyond dreams, the sleep your bones acknowledge only because hours have passed and you remember nothing, the only sleep that matters. No. At two o'clock in the morning I am profoundly awake. I slip downstairs and out the front door. I sit in the porch swing, drinking scotch and listening to the birds call to each other, or to themselves.

Two years ago—before I habitually used words like *volatile* and *tenuous* and *disease,* before I could hear the dry cells cracking beneath my skin, before I became suddenly old—I would have said the birds were calling to me. But now I sit just beyond the periphery of things. Now it's me, a cold moon, revolving around the world.

Glenna does not know about birds singing at night because (1) she sleeps and (2) I have never told her. If I said, "Glenna, birds sing always, even at two in the morning," she would jab her slender hands against her curved hips and shout, "What the hell are you doing up at two A.M., Sylvia?" And because I still believe in honesty, I would have to answer, "Sitting in the porch swing, drinking scotch and listening to the birds sing." And Glenna's blue eyes would sweat with rage, and her pretty mouth would twitch, and she'd shout, "Where in hell did you get the scotch, Sylvia?" And because I still believe in honesty, I would have to answer, "From a shoe box hidden in the back of my closet." And Glenna would roll her sweaty blue eyes toward heaven and shout (the only volume she uses with me), "Christ, Sylvia!" She would then storm upstairs, throw open my closet door and dig through the pile of treasures she calls junk until she found the criminal shoe box. She would carry the bottle of scotch to the bathroom with two fingers as if it were something vile and pour the contents into the toilet. And there would be more threats about sending me back to Saint-Just Hospital. And without the scotch I would never be able to sleep again, not even the imperfect sleep of dreams. And the subject of birds singing at night would be lost forever. So it's just as well Glenna remains ignorant of matters which to her have no significance anyway.

Two nights ago, as I lay in bed waiting for Glenna to fall asleep, waiting with one eye cocked on the closet door, I heard a cat die. The horrible, pained laments rose from the street below my window very slowly, spreading wide into the night air. At first they resembled the feverish cries of an infant—colicky, sporadic. Then they grew louder, more urgent, lengthening with each higher octave. Then they did not stop: a cat screaming in imponderable anguish, filling up my room, the street, the entire silent neighborhood with its banshee shrieks.

I lay stunned in the dark, unmoving, for fear that whatever demon was torturing the cat would certainly find me, too. And then it stopped. Too abruptly. As if the screams literally had been ripped from the cat's throat.

The silence returned. I got out of bed and walked, trembling, to Glenna's room, quietly knocked on the door and let myself in.

Glenna bolted upright, swaying from half-sleep.

"Did you hear it?" I asked.

"Hear what?"

"The cat."

"What cat?"

"There was a cat screaming in the street below."

"I didn't hear a thing."

"It was horrible, Glenna. Deafening."

"You were dreaming."

"I was awake."

"Then you were hallucinating."

"It was real. And gruesome."

"Go back to bed, Sylvia."

I took one step into the room. "Glenna?"

"For chrissake, *what?*"

"I know you won't understand this, probably are not able to comprehend this, but it sounded as if the cat were being eaten alive. Very slowly, Glenna."

She leaned suddenly toward me, and I could feel the bristling of her rage as she hissed, "Get the hell out of my room, you goddamn freak."

Yet my sister, for all her exquisitely-packaged stupidity, may be right about my rambling, my *digression*—her borrowed word, the word she borrowed from Dr Warren, who was the first to use it in reference to my *condition*—my borrowed word, the word I will gladly give back to Dr Warren after this story has been written. It is, I'm sure, the wrong word. It conjures up images of skin rashes or palsied hands rather than a mind that moves too quickly for language.

The last time I saw Dr Warren he said *digression* and *condition* in the same sentence. I sat in the hall just outside his office and heard him tell Glenna: "You will find that Sylvia's condition often causes digression."

I was not impressed.

Glenna was impressed. She lowered her voice two octaves; from fifteen feet away I could smell the sudden heat of her body as she shifted her legs to a more seductive pose.

"Digression?" beautiful Glenna asked wealthy Dr Warren. (The adjectives here are crucial.)

"Yes," said Dr Warren. "Digression."

Pause. The vapid eyes remained vapid.

"Rambling, Glenna."

Pause. Perhaps a slight curl of the painted lips, but nothing more.

"Wandering from one subject to another without any sense of direction."

"Oh!" Glenna comprehended. (A memorable moment.)

The nurse who sat with me in the hall chain-smoked and read a women's magazine. I asked her for a cigarette. She handed it to me without raising her eyes from the pasta recipes. I smoked and watched a silverfish skate across the floor. I listened:

"Now, Glenna . . . You don't mind if I call you Glenna, do you?"

"No. I'd like that very much."

"Glenna. I want you—" (Yes, I knew he already did.) "—to keep Sylvia on course when she's speaking. Don't let her become sidetracked and begin talking about insects, for example."

"Insects?"

And I thought: Yes, insects, Glenna. Dung beetles, wolf spiders, horseflies, termites, millipedes, mud daubers, tarantulas . . .

Tarantula. *Eurypelma californicum.*

In the desert the male tarantula seeks the female. When he finds her she is angry, hungry for the kill. But he must mate with her; he has no choice. It is nature, survival of a species, proliferation of an organism that does not even know its name.

He carries his semen in a sac at the base of his front legs. He must plant the semen in a pouch of the female's belly. She is reclusive by nature, malevolent. She wants to kill him, and he has no choice.

They lunge toward each other in a violent dance of instincts. He unfolds two long fangs from his head and wields them like tusks, keeping the female's poisonous bite away from his delicate membranes. He takes the advantage. He positions the fangs just below hers. She struggles while he lifts her up so that the pouch of her belly, the one that holds hundreds of infertile eggs, is laid bare. He quickly rams his feet inside the pouch and deposits his semen.

This is the moment they have lived for, the only reason they're alive. It is the same inevitable circumstance that brought them into existence—so they could later re-create their own conceptions. They have come full circle now. But for the male, the circle is his final geometry: the moment he withdraws his empty sacs from her belly and attempts a retreat, she will strike out and plunge her deadly fangs into his vulnerable flesh. He will fall, stunned. And she will eat him alive, needing her strength for all the young tarantulas now growing inside her belly.

So much for love in the desert.

That day, one month ago, my last day at Saint-Just: The nurse pulled a pen from the pocket of her uniform and began taking a magazine quiz, "Are You a Good Listener?" The ubiquitous silverfish crawled across the toe of her shoe.

Dr Warren said, "Insects, politics, dolphins, God. Anything that isn't related to the subject she started with."

And I thought: They are all related, Dr Warren: Insects, politics, dolphins, God. And all are relevant to everything else. Everything. That's the way I see it; that's the way it is.

Glenna asked, "Why?" And did she lean toward Dr Warren just then, the neckline of her sweater falling away to reveal her swollen breasts?

Probably: Dr Warren cleared his throat. "Well, you see, Glenna, your sister must learn to organize her thought patterns. Develop them into some sort of rational sequence. Once she learns to do this, we're hoping she'll be able to organize her life in the same way. Of course, it's purely conjecture. Yet there's a chance she'll be one step closer to leading a normal existence."

"Normal?" (A good question for a Glenna to ask a Dr Warren.)

"Yes, Glenna. Normal. Like you. Like me."

Ha! That's what I thought. Or perhaps I said it aloud, because the nurse snapped her head around and narrowed her eyes at me. She stomped her cigarette out on the floor—and with it the lovely silverfish—then laid the magazine aside and closed the door to Dr Warren's office. But she was too late. I had already heard him tell Glenna about the rambling, the *digression*. Had already imagined the slow intercourse building between them. Had already considered the consequences of leading a normal life. Like Glenna. Like Dr Warren.

Oh, god.

Now I live with Glenna. During the day I sit in the small room she has assigned me, reading the encyclopedia and listening to Rampal. At night I listen to birds.

Dr Warren phones for Glenna every day. Although he does not say, "This is Dr Warren calling," I know it's him. For over a year I listened to that dull, controlled voice until it became a soundtrack I could not turn off, not even during sleep. It swept through my marrow, sat trembling on my nerve endings, gnawed at the base of my skull. When I remembered old lovers and smiled at the memories, the voice said: *That's all past, Sylvia. What about today? Where are you today, Sylvia?* The smiles vanished. Of course it's Dr Warren who's calling.

This morning Glenna took the phone from me and waved me out of the room. I climbed the stairs to my small bedroom, feeling no need to eavesdrop. I knew the dialogue: She would make plans to meet Dr Warren in the city. They would have lunch and then go to a hotel. Or skip lunch altogether. Glenna would wrap her long legs around Dr Warren and draw him inside her, draw him in so deeply that he would never want to leave. He would become lost in that warm dark envelope of Glenna's sex and be glad about it. This is how Glenna operates.

Glenna is a professional ex-wife. That's how she acquired this house, the neglected Motherwell, Chagall, and Miro prints, the Jaguar in the garage, the insured wardrobe. She has been married four times. Two were doctors, one a lawyer, the last owned a chain of drugstores. To become as wealthy as Glenna does not take intelligence. It requires only a lack of scruples and a smoldering crotch. Glenna possesses both in extraordinary proportions.

Yesterday I heard her weeping into the phone and then, moments later, laughing to herself in the bedroom. She is moving in for the kill. Dr Warren is her next victim. I will be the innocent bystander.

The clinical term for my condition is *undifferentiated schizophrenia*. At least that's what Dr Warren said. And so he also wrote in my file, which I stole from his office one afternoon many months ago, and read while sitting in the white sterile toilet of my Saint-Just suite. The file cited various psychologists and psychiatrists and their respective books. Books which were contained in Dr Warren's office library. Which I eventually stole, one by one, returning one before stealing another, and read in the white sterile toilet. And understood.

The certain causes of schizophrenia are unknown. There is no certain cure. None of this surprises me. Let Dr Warren, let Glenna, be surprised:

I have never been insane. My condition has always been, will always be, knowing too much. Knowing, especially, that love is fragile, but not as fragile as those who love.

Two years ago a man who loved me drove his car off the side of a mountain, and I began speaking about whales. Great blue

whales who bear their young off the coast of the Valdez
Peninsula. Every year, during the South American spring, they
swim thousands of miles to find that one spot of the world. The
same spot their ancestors were drawn to year after year. Ages
ago. When "spring" was nothing but a trigger in the womb,
pulled by a steady omnipotent finger. Thousands of miles. And
behind the great blues come the dolphins. And behind the dolphins come the killer whales who are there only to devour the
newborn calves. The dolphins come only to prevent the
slaughter. They have nothing to gain, everything to lose. They
are altruism at its best.

It's the dolphins who are significant to the story.

Glenna says *this* story is my last chance. She says if I cannot stick
to one subject without digressing, if I cannot make my point
clearly and simply and logically, then she will send me back to
Saint-Just.

It doesn't matter. She will send me back, digression or not.

In a hotel bed, she will convince Dr Warren that my condition has worsened. Still moving inside her, Dr Warren will
agree, then ask her to marry him. She will say yes. They will get
married. Six months to a year later, Glenna will refuse him sex.
He will complain, then grow angry, then have an affair. Glenna
will sue him for divorce on grounds of infidelity.

Glenna's next house will be bigger, in a better neighborhood.

The last conversation Glenna and I had was about . . . what?

We were walking in her garden, a beautiful garden going bad
from the usual neglect. I pointed to an enormous oak—ancient,
dignified—and asked, "How old would you say that tree is?"

And Glenna said, "I don't know. Too old. Too goddamn big."

"It is big," I smiled.

"Too big," said Glenna, frowning. "It's coming down next
week."

"Coming down?"

"I'm having it removed."

"I see."

"It puts too much shade on the terrace there. I can't sun-bathe after three in the afternoon. And the leaves! Christ, what a mess!" She kicked her leather sandals through a thin blanket of leaves left over from last season.

I walked up to the oak and put the flat of my palm against its rough bark. I said, "A hundred years, perhaps. Perhaps more. Such a long, long time."

Glenna looked at me and squinted, "What the hell are you talking about?"

And I remember thinking then about the beginning of the world. About how the dinosaurs came slowly up and out of the primeval ooze and lived for millions of years, nibbling leaves off the tops of trees resembling that oak. Trees no larger or smaller than they should have been for their purpose. And then the dinosaurs died off, and the trees remained, still growing tall. And then I considered the size of things: the large fauna and flora still left in this world—large only because we, *homo sapiens,* are so small. Like the redwoods, old oaks and elms, giraffes, whales, elephants . . .

And so I turned suddenly to Glenna and I asked: "Why is it, Glenna, that the woolly mammoth fell to extinction and the elephant, its close kin, did not?"

And Glenna cautiously stepped toward me, her eyes wide, perhaps afraid, and she said, "Sylvia. You're digressing."

A month passes and what you remember is the night. It doesn't rain. The grass is pale and dry. The worms crawl deeper into the earth, and the birds lament this fact, refuse sleep because of it. They, and everyone else who knows the condition of this sea-son, are hungry.

So you sit in the porch swing, drinking scotch until your hands grow numb, writing a story that becomes more and more illegible.

And the birds sing.

And your life—the only one you know—goes on forever, swallowing darkness and spitting up the memories that brought you here.

(I loved the man who died at the foot of the mountain. His heart was so full of goodness, he could not find room for the world's pain.)

So let this story be about dolphins, Glenna. Let it be about the woolly mammoth. About the last painful cries of cats. About all the species and subspecies who are, in one way or another, marching toward their own extinctions.

Let it be, finally, about love . . . and desert love . . .

You will say I'm digressing, Glenna, but there is so much you do not know.

Drowning Hard

I ONCE TOLD JOEY I wasn't as pretty as he wanted me to be, and he said, "It's the inside of you I care about." Well, I thought he was referring to my heart, its kindness and generosity, but what he really meant was my sex, its tightness and generosity.

I am a big woman with big feet and square hands. My sex is a contradiction. It's small. Joey says it's like a virgin's. A fifteen-year-old virgin's to be exact. How the hell would he know? The first time he had sex was with a thirty-eight-year-old truck driver he met at a roadside honky-tonk coming back from a skiing trip in Aspen, and she sure as hell was no virgin. In one night she taught him more about a woman's body than most men learn their whole lives, sad but true. Joey was just nineteen then and slumming, something he could do because he grew up not rich exactly, but very comfortable. His dad's a successful ob-gyn, a fact which makes Joey think himself an expert on vaginas by way of genealogy.

I've never had the luxury of going slumming since I grew up not poor exactly, but semideprived. My dad was a plumber who worked only when he damned well felt like it, and he did not damn well feel like it very often. If I were the poetic type who trusted the validity of metaphors, I might say my father's occupation would make me an authority on male plumbing. But I am not poetic and therefore do not consider myself a penis expert. I only know what feels good and what feels right and that only half of the goodness and rightness is directly attributable to a penis's length or width. The other half is the result of what's inside. And I mean the heart, its kindness and generosity.

You'd think that a man who tells a woman all he really cares about is her sex would lack that inside half which excuses whatever may be lacking in genital endowment. But that's not entirely the case with Joey. His heart is okay, though you can't see its okayness if you're looking at him straight on. Straight on he's too handsome for his own good. His handsomeness is the first and last thing you notice about him if you haven't learned to look elsewhere. I've learned. Joey taught me.

On cloudless, moonless nights we go out and lie on our backs in his yard, counting stars. There are millions. And there's this phenomenon that makes some invisible unless you look at them obliquely because they're more distant, their light dimmed by the brilliance of closer stars.

"But that doesn't mean they're not burning just as brightly," says Joey, "relative to their place in the cosmic scheme of things."

Like me, he implies, *distant but still shining.*

Sure, Joey shines. He has his moments. And most of them are in bed. Actually, there are two things Joey does well. One is screwing, the other is swimming.

I've seen him in an ocean where the waves were too high, too fierce, the water breaking hard onto the shore, swallowing gluttonous bites of beach with the foamy teeth of its ebb and flow. And there'd be Joey: floating like a new bobber, turning backward somersaults and flinging his arms up unafraid as the waves rolled under him and raised him high toward the blue ceiling of heaven. Sometimes they'd swallow him too, taking him down into their angry depths, tumbling him head over heels far below the surface while I'd watch, not breathing, waiting for him to emerge. And he'd burst through the surface, laughing hard, that confident shit-eating grin on his face that says water is his element, that he will always rise to the surface, come out on top, no matter how rough it gets.

In bed it's the same.

As I said, I'm a big woman. I can roll him like an ocean beneath the convoluted sheets, flipping him over onto his back and holding him under with the strength of my thighs, enveloping him in my own salty wetness. The difference is, I can drown him. I can make him gasp for air and cry out to God and Jesus— not for mercy, but to let them know he's coming.

When I have rolled him from one end of the bed to the other, sometimes rolled him onto the floor, flipped him this way and that without once letting him slip out of me so that I grow hot as a car seat in summer, I grab hold of his shoulders and push him down, clench his loins with my knees and ride him slow and easy, while his eyes glaze over like just before dying, watching mine, waiting for them to glaze too, narrow to slits, roll up inside my head which tells him he can stop holding back, aim for that divine destination deep inside my sex and notify God or Jesus that his moment has indeed arrived.

I do not wish to imply that our relationship is purely sexual. We talk. We wax philosophically about a hundred different things, none of which include love. Love is not practical for us. It complicates things. Unlike lust which is straightforward and easy to accommodate. The problem is, I don't fit into Joey's world the way I fit into his bed. I know this. Deep down inside, Joey knows it, too.

Not so long ago he was blinded by lust, made incredibly stupid because his brain was concentrating all of its efforts on his penis, which is not a particularly rational part of the male anatomy. Blind and stupid, he invited me to a party at the country club. I said no. He asked why not. I said, "Look at me, Joey. The size of my feet, the squareness of my hands."

"The tightness of your sex," he replied.

"Who the hell's going to see that?"

"I will," he said, "even when you're wearing clothes."

Temporarily made blind and stupid by his confession of desire, I relented.

The party was being held in honor of his parents' thirtieth wedding anniversary. A hundred people showed up. Doctors, lawyers, bankers. And their wives whose vaginas had been examined at one time or another by Joey's father. And their children who had plopped out of those vaginas and into the doctor's hands. They were all remarkably pretty, remarkably handsome, like Joey. Their hands were not square.

Joey's parents rushed us the moment we stepped through the door. His father looked at me and said, "Well, well!" His mother nodded, "So *this* is the girl who's been occupying my son's life."

Your son's bed, I wanted to say, but just smiled.

Joey smiled, too, like he was actually proud to have me with him, though it was most likely the pride of his penis smiling.

It was a long night. People asked me questions. They wanted to know what my father did for a living. I told them, "Nothing." And when they blinked their eyes once and slowly, I added, "He's dead." They wanted to know if I was related to so-and-so of such-and-such fame, how Joey and I had met, how long I had known Joey, where I'd gone to school, if I had trouble finding stylish shoes in my size.

Joey did not hear the questions—or the answers, which were not the ones I wanted to give but the ones I gave for Joey's sake. He did not hear them because he was always halfway across the room at the time, cornered by some old fart slapping him on the back and talking nonstop in his face while Joey nodded and drank, looking at me over the rim of his glass and winking.

I'd drunk plenty myself, so when I went to the bathroom and heard one woman who was pissing ask another woman who was pissing, "What in the world does Joey see in her," I answered, "My sex. Its tightness and generosity." Their pissing abruptly stopped. They did not speak or quit squeezing until they were sure I had walked out of the bathroom. But I hung around outside the door just long enough to hear them say, in unison, "The little slut," just as they let go of their pee.

I walked back to the party and straight up to Joey and pressed my lips against his ear and whispered, "Dance with me."

He said, "But no one else is dancing."

I said, "I know. That's the point."

He smiled at me and gave me that look of his, the one he gives me each time I reach for his zipper that cages the wild beast of his excitement. He slipped his arm beneath mine as if I were a princess and led me to the middle of the dance floor, wrapped one arm around my waist, laced his fingers through mine and brought the square clump of my hand to his cheek. Our feet did not move, but we swayed side to side, groins pressed tight and growing hot against one another, some old tearjerker tune playing in the background, and Joey and me staring into each other's eyes like two characters in a black-and-white movie.

For a long while everybody just stood there watching us, their drinks held in awkward incomplete gestures, their mouths still gaping from unfinished sentences. Then the women began to stare at their husbands with squinty eyes as if searching for something they'd left behind, something that the distance of time had made small and therefore hard to see when they looked at it straight on. And the husbands turned to catch these searching stares and were for a moment bewildered, until they looked again at Joey and me and understood and perhaps also remembered because they set down their drinks and smiled at their wives and slowly led them out onto the dance floor.

Since that night, Joey has asked me to every party that comes along, even though I fight the stupid blindness of my libido, and win, and always tell him no. He eventually heard about the questions I answered that night, heard I'm sure a lot of other questions from his father and mother who shook my square hands as we were leaving their party and said, "Perhaps we'll see you again," hoping they never would.

It took me a while, but I finally convinced Joey to take other women to those parties, pretty women with slender hands and small feet, who do not mind all the questions because they have all the right answers. So he takes them to the parties and afterward he takes them home. Then he comes over to my place and we screw like it's the last chance we'll ever have. Which it will be, someday.

Jocy had a party just last night. It was his birthday party. He's twenty-eight now. After midnight came and he was officially a year older and everyone had kissed him and slapped him on the back, he waited a half-hour, then pretended to feel sick and sent everybody packing. Fifteen minutes later, he was at my place, diving into my steamy waters. Though he was pretty drunk, it didn't affect his performance any. He stayed hard for a whole hour while I rolled him especially fierce since it was, after all, his birthday—my gift to him. But this time when he came he didn't call out to God or Jesus, he called out to me: flailing his arms over his head, bucking against the tide of my heat, screaming out my name like a drowning man drowning hard, going under for the very last time.

Afterward he lay on his back, staring at the ceiling. I raised myself up on one elbow and looked down at him and said, "You know, it doesn't bother me that I'm not as pretty as you want me to be."

And he said, "I've told you before, it's the inside of you I care about."

"Right," I smiled, "my sex. Its tightness and generosity."

He looked up at me and frowned, then grabbed hold of my hand, yanked me to my feet and led me out onto the deck of my apartment, the old wood already cool and wet with night. He pointed at the big sky above us and said, "Tell me how many stars there are."

"Millions," I replied.

"And how many of them are shining?" he asked, "how many of them burn?" His voice was hoarse and low like he'd spent the whole day and night yelling at a football game, and I knew he was crying.

I had never seen Joey cry before and did not want to see him cry now because just the thought of it made my heart drop inside my chest like a stone cracked and falling. So I looked down at my hands—at my big square hands that maybe were not pretty with their rough palms and short fingers and chewed nails but were strong and useful nevertheless—and I laid them on Joey's shoulders to stop the awful trembling there and pressed myself tight against his back and leaned my head in close to whisper, "They all shine, Joey."

He gasped a little, a pitiful kind of sob, and then sighed. "Do we?"

I nodded and smiled. "Sure, baby. Relative to our place in the cosmic scheme of things, we're all burning."

An Interview with My Husband

JAVIER AGREES TO THE INTERVIEW with some reluctance. He has just returned from a month-long visit to see his family, et al., in Argentina. *Just* means three days ago. For three days he has spoken to no one. Except to say that he is muy cansado—very tired. Except to say, sadly, that the city looks the same, the apartment looks the same, I look the same. For three days I have endured the silence, chalking it up to a period of cultural readjustment.

DAY NUMBER 3

ME: Javier, let's have a little talk.

JAVIER: I don't like little talks.

ME: Then let's call it an interview.

JAVIER: (Eyes squint, eyebrows raise. A typical somewhat seductive gesture for a detective in a cheap murder mystery. But Javier is no detective; he's my husband, and I know that look like I know the sound of fingers absently tapping on the kitchen table.)

Look at him. He is magnificent with his black hair and black eyes and skin the color of a young fawn. And me? I am blonde and pale. My eyes are blue and wet with a perpetual sexual hunger. And maybe there are lines around those eyes, but only when I smile—which is not as often as it used to be.

Here is the difference: Javier is twenty-three. I am thirty. Still, when we walk down the street together, no one whispers behind our backs, no one points. But give it time.

ME: An interview, Javier. You know. I'll be the objective reporter and you the celebrity. We've played the game before, remember? A year ago. Right before we were married. When your English stunk. Before I made you what you are today—fluent, gainfully employed, smug. Wasn't it fun, Javier?

JAVIER: (Shoulders shrug.)

ME: Yes or no.

JAVIER: Okay. But there is one specific.

ME: *Specification.*

JAVIER: Specification.

ME: What is it?

JAVIER: The interview must be given in the place I want it to be given.

ME: (Cautious smile.) And where might that be, love?

JAVIER: (Unrestrained sneer.) On the roof.

I am afraid of heights. Javier knows this.

Our apartment is on the top floor of an old three-story mansion. The roof can be reached only by climbing out our bathroom window, shuffling across fifteen feet of a two-foot-wide catwalk, then crawling up a steep gable to the roof's apex—which is not less than fifty feet above the ground. It can be a dangerous trek for someone suffering from vertigo. I suffer from vertigo. Javier does not know the meaning of vertigo. He has jumped out of airplanes, scaled perfectly vertical cliffs, gone hang-gliding, and climbed to the roof at least once a week for as long as he has lived with me.

What does Javier do on the roof? Sing? Dream? Masturbate? Who knows? My curiosity has never been great enough to overcome my fear.

ME: Give me a break, Javier.

JAVIER: (Unrelenting sneer.) A good reporter will do anything
         for a story.

ME: Is that so.

JAVIER: Yes. (Walking toward the bathroom.) Are you coming?
         Rule number one: Do not keep a celebrity waiting. Ha
         ha ha.

ME: (Graciously.) Fuck off.

JAVIER: (Calling from the bathroom.) And don't forget to bring
         your tape recorder!

WHAT I DID DURING JAVIER'S ABSENCE:

1 Went, alone, to every matinee at the Foreign Film Cinema and wept
   (tragedies and comedies alike). I sat through the credits until the
   lights came up, until everyone else had left the theater, until the red
   had drained from my eyes and I could walk out into the revealing
   afternoon light without embarrassment.

2 Went to the zoo and fed fish to the sea lions until my fingers smelled like the deck of an ocean trawler marooned under a hot sun.

3 Took long baths and counted the bathroom tiles. (There are 352.)

4 Waited for the telephone to ring.

5 Finished a fifth of Johnny Walker Red all by myself.

6 Waited for the telephone to ring.

7 Sent four telexes to Argentina. ($77.93 plus tax.)

8 Waited for the telephone to ring.

9 Missed Javier and waited for the telephone to ring. (The telephone
   never rang.)

JAVIER: (Loudly, from above.) Time passes quickly! Opportun-
         ities are missed!

ME: The least you could do is give me a hand!

JAVIER: How badly do you want it?

ME: What—the hand?

JAVIER: No, the interview! How badly do you want it?

ME: I want it, you coelenterate! Help me!

JAVIER: (Possibly, very wicked laughter.)

ME: You're a son of a bitch, you know that? If I fall, you will
           have to bear the weight of that burden throughout
           your life!

JAVIER: Son of a bitch? S-s-selen-selentrate? Tsk-tsk-tsk. Rule
           number two: A reporter must be objective at all time.

ME: At all *times!* With an S! And here's objective for you:
           You are a sadistic sonofabitching coelenterate!

JAVIER: (Head peering around the gable, across fifteen feet of
           catwalk, at me who is standing just outside the bath-
           room window, my body pressed flat as a salamander's
           against the side of the house.) Well?

ME: Well what?

JAVIER: Well, you look ridiculous and—how can I say it?—
           without protection.

ME: Vulnerable?

JAVIER: Sure, vulnerable. (Lecherous grin.) Suddenly I feel very
           excited.

The first time Javier and I made love was the first time I had a
multiple orgasm. It wasn't that Javier was so incredibly adept—
although he does tend to move well, to slide his hands over the
right places at precisely the right times, to shift gears with the
precision of an Indy 500 winner. No, I think the multiple orgasm had everything to do with the difference in our ages. It is
erotic going to bed with a man who is three years younger than
your youngest brother. It smacks of incest, of the Oedipus
complex, of statutory rape, of a Great Transgression, of a viola-
tion of a commandment Moses neglected to bring down from
the mountain. And the forbidden always tastes a little sweeter,
doesn't it? Honestly, isn't it more exciting screwing in a public
toilet than in your own bedroom?

WHAT I DID DURING JAVIER'S ABSENCE:
(*addendum*)

10 Made a list of all the places where Javier and I had made love. (The
     bathtub, the coffee table, the front steps at 2:00 A.M., the back steps

at 8:00 P.M., the hood of our neighbor's car at 6:30 A.M., the swimming area of Lake Tapikka—half submerged—the toilet of Loo's Jap-
anese Restaurant—*oh!* And, of course, our bedroom.)

ME: Forget it, Javier. I wouldn't be able to concentrate.
JAVIER: You have to concentrate to have sex?
ME: Certainly. I have to concentrate on where I am, where
         my body is, so that when I climax I can feel myself van-
         ishing.
JAVIER: That's the stupidest thing I have ever heard.
ME: The *most stupid.*
JAVIER: Exactly. (Pained sigh.) There is no justification for the
         young.
ME: No *justice* for the young. Although you may have been
         right the first time.

No one came to our wedding. No one came because no one
was invited. The marriage was a spontaneous decision, made
during a Saturday afternoon chess game.

I said: *Life would be easier if you were working.*

And Javier said: *I'm here on a student visa. I can't work.*

And I said: *If we got married you would be legal, you could work.*

And Javier said: *I can't marry you because I'm in love with you.*
Check.

And I said: *What the hell are you talking about?*

And Javier said: *I think you take marriage too seriously, so if I*
marry you I might hurt you someday.

And I said: *Bullshit. I don't take marriage too seriously, and you*
will hurt me someday with or without a marriage license.

And Javier said: *Okay. We'll get married. Checkmate.*

Four days later we went to the courthouse alone and were
married in a three-minute ceremony by a judge who mech-
anically wished us the best of luck in all the world and hoped
he wouldn't see us again in divorce court. Afterward, I was
surprised that nothing had changed, that I looked and felt
exactly the same.

Javier watched me staring at my reflection and said: *So what did you expect?*

And I said: *I don't know. Something.*

And Javier said: *It's what I told you. You take marriage too seriously.*

And I said: *It's just a piece of paper.*

And Javier said: *Keep telling yourself that and maybe you will believe it someday.*

JAVIER: Shit! Open your eyes or we will both fall!

ME: I can't!

JAVIER: Don't be a stupid! Open your eyes! You're going to walk off the edge!

ME: I can't do it, Javier.

JAVIER: Vieja, vieja! Open your eyes!

ME: (Eyes open, slit thin as a cat's about to pounce.) Don't ever call me old woman again.

JAVIER: (A politician's smile.) But now your eyes are open, yes?

ME: Why did you call mc vieja?

JAVIER: Look, mi estrellita! Only a few more steps to the top!

ME: Javier, do you think of me as an old woman?

JAVIER: Please. No questions until the interview.

All of Javier's friends are at least seven years younger than me. When they visit, they sit on the floor with legs nimbly crossed at the ankles and wear a look of arrogance that says they believe they will live forever. My friends, on the other hand, sit in straight-backed chairs with their feet flat on the floor and their hands clutching the chair's arm, or a cigarette, or a glass of scotch, and in their eyes shines a cold light of stifled desperation, and in their voices trills a cynicism barely disguised: They have already seen their own deaths—once, twice, maybe more —in nightmares from which they wake sweating and cold. And when both groups of friends are in the same room together they pass between each other, respectively:

1 the arrogant laughter and cocky smiles, and
2 the subtle arrows of resentment aimed at the youthful ignorance
   they would give their right arms to have again.

JAVIER: (Standing, legs straddling the peak of the roof.) See? It
          was not so difficult, was it?

ME: (Lying prone on the westward slope, eyes shut tight
          against the wide sky.) My god, I'm going to faint.

JAVIER: You can see for many miles from this roof. Look! Over
          there is the radio tower. There is only one tree taller
          than me at this moment.

ME: I'm very happy for you.

JAVIER: So are you ready to begin? I am ready. I feel like God,
          and I can answer any question you ask.

ME: (Eyes open briefly to find the RECORD button.) Okay,
          God, we begin . . . *now.* Who are you?

JAVIER: I am Javier Ricardo Girolamo.

ME: That's only your name. Who are you?

JAVIER: I don't understand.

ME: You are twenty-three years old. You must have some
          idea of who you are.

JAVIER: (Silence.)

ME: Who are you?

JAVIER: (Hesitating.) My father was born in Italy and my
          mother was born—

ME: I'm not asking for your family history. I don't want to
          know about your mother or father or sisters or brothers.
          I want to know who you are.

JAVIER: (Unattractive petulance.) Go to the next question,
          please.

Less than a year ago, shortly after Javier and I were married,
immediately after we'd made love on the living room floor, I
straddled Javier's ass and began massaging his back and asked:
Does it bother you much that I'm seven years older than you?

And Javier said: *Age is not important. I would not love you more if you was younger.*

And I said: Were *younger. If you* were *younger.*

And Javier said: *Were younger. I love you for who you are at this moment.*

And I asked: *Who am I, Javier?*

And Javier said: *You are the woman I love.*

And I said: *Javier, someday you will have to answer who you are to know who I am because, as you say, I am the woman you love.*

And Javier said: *Please rub a little lower on that side.*

ME: (Eyes still closed, the vertigo passing.) Javier Ricardo Girolamo, do you love your wife?

JAVIER: Wife? What does this mean? It is only a word for the woman who has signed a paper with a man who will be called husband by the stupids who can see nothing but the word marriage. Wife is only a word. It has a small definition. So. That is not a very good question, do you think?

ME: All right then. This woman you have married and have lived with for more than one year—do you love her?

JAVIER: I think so. I . . . um . . . Sure, I love her.

ME: (Eyes open wide now, head turned toward Javier who is sitting on the apex of the roof, hands on knees, staring out across space like a calm sentinel.) Why do you hesitate?

JAVIER: I don't know. I am very confused right now. I have just come from my home in Argentina. I am very confused.

ME: You are confused about whether or not you love your wife?

JAVIER: No. I am sure I love my wife—if you have to use this word. But I am just not sure of *how* I love my wife.

The week before Javier left for Argentina was perhaps the best week of our life together. We were very close then. We made love every day, slowly spinning on the bed like two syncopated gyroscopes. We talked about senseless and poignant things. We talked, too, about the year we had spent together and how good it had been. We agreed that we had no regrets.

The day of Javier's departure, at the airport, I felt as if my lungs were slowly being sucked out of my body. I couldn't breathe. My voice was small and fragile.

Javier touched my hair and my face and said: *Amor de mi vida, you can't know how much I love you at this moment.*

And I said: *Please tell me.*

And Javier said: *I love you ten millions of times more than you can imagine.*

And I said: *Ten* million *times, without the* S, *without the* of.

ME: Describe your wife to me.
JAVIER: She is very beautiful—(Quick grin.)—for a woman who is thirty years old.
ME: (Objectively.) Go to hell.
JAVIER: She is also very intelligent. She tells this to everyone.
ME: No, she does not tell this to everyone.
JAVIER: How can you know? You are only a reporter. Can I finish?
ME: I don't know, *can* you?
JAVIER: *May* I finish?
ME: Please do.
JAVIER: She has a good heart most of the times—
ME: *Time.* Most of the *time.* No S.
JAVIER: Please! If you keep to stop me we will—
ME: Keep *stopping* me. No *to,* with an I-N-G on the—
JAVIER: (Hands thrown up in what I presume to be a sign of disgust.) Shut up! Shut up!
ME: I'm only trying to educate you in the English language.
JAVIER: I know. I appreciate you to teach me—
ME: (Biting the tongue.)
JAVIER: —but we will never finish the interview this way.

ME: Okay, I apologize.

JAVIER: Now. I was telling you . . . What was I telling you?

ME: That I . . . that *your wife* has a good heart. Most of the time.

JAVIER: Yes. I think she always has a good heart but sometimes
         she forgets about it. Sometimes she is like a child. She
         cries about her life. She gets depression about her life
         too much. She forgets that her life is very easy in the
         United States. She forgets sometimes that she is not the
         only person in the world and that her life is very easy
         here. She tells people she is intelligent because she
         knows it is true. Sometimes I feel like a stupid when we
         talk. She is maybe the most incredible woman I have
         known in my life. Did I say she is very beautiful?

ME: Yes. Thank you.

JAVIER: What else do you want to know about her?

ME: Nothing else. You've done a good job.

Some time ago, while Javier and I were having dinner at a dull
restaurant, we had a very interesting conversation. It was about
sex, of course. About each and every sexual encounter we'd had
up to that point. Javier described each woman he'd made love
with, each sexual position he'd held, each strange combination
he'd participated in. He talked for five minutes. When it was my
turn, I had a difficult time remembering all the men I'd slept
with. The positions sounded like the text of a sex manual. The
combinations seemed infinite. I talked for over twenty minutes,
and each minute Javier's countenance grew more despairing.
By the time I had finished, he was slumped in his chair, his eyes
glassy and staring through me at some invisible object of desire
a thousand miles away.

  I said: *I have experienced a lot in my time, haven't I?*

  And Javier said: *In my time I have experienced a lot, also, but my
time is much shorter than yours.*

  And I said: *I am acutely aware of that fact.*

———

ME: Javier, tell me what happened in Argentina.

JAVIER: What do you mean?

ME: What happened in Argentina that caused you to become so confused?

JAVIER: Nothing of much signification.

ME: *Significance.*

JAVIER: (Scowl.)

ME: I'm sorry. Old habits die hard.

JAVIER: (Scowl.)

ME: I promise I won't do it again. So what happened in Argentina?

JAVIER: I saw my family. I saw my friends. I had a very good time with my family and my friends. I considered my life in this country that is so different from my life in Argentina.

ME: In what way is it so different?

JAVIER: I can't explain. It is only that Argentina is Argentina. The United States is someplace else.

There were only a few times during the year Javier lived with me that he became homesick for Argentina. Once was after a party where he got very drunk. He had wanted to play some Argentine music on the stereo. And he played the music, and he translated the words of the first song for everyone, and no one listened. After the song ended, he calmly removed the record from the turntable and threw it against a wall and walked out. When I arrived home, I found him sitting in the bathtub drinking Argentine wine, reading Julio Cortázar and listening, at full volume, to gaucho ballads.

I asked: *What's the matter, Javier?*

And Javier said: *Sometimes I think I could leave this place tomorrow.*

And I said: *Some time, I think, you will leave this place tomorrow.*

ME: Javier, there must have been something that happened in Argentina, some specific incident, that changed you.

JAVIER: I am the same as before.

ME: No, you are not the same. When you stepped off the
         plane at the airport, your wife was very happy to see
         you. She ran up to you and embraced you, but your
         arms hung at your sides like ballasts.

JAVIER: I was very tired. What is ballast?

ME: Never mind. Can a person be so tired that he cannot
         return the embrace of the person he loves, who loves
         him back?

JAVIER: I was tired. I don't know about other people who love.

ME: Do you know about yourself who loves?

JAVIER: These are stupid questions.

ME: No, they are simply questions.

JAVIER: (Silence.)

The day Javier was to arrive at the airport, I felt two emotions:

1 *anger,* because he had not called during his absence, because he had
   ignored the impassioned telexes that described my loneliness and
   pain in rather excesssive detail, and

2 *joy,* simply because he was returning, because I had envisioned his
   return for five weeks, because I believed it would be the final reso-
   lution of our relationship, a confirmation that *because he was returning* he belonged with me (to me?)—not with whomever or whatever
   kept pulling him back to Argentina.

His flight was delayed twice. With each delay my anxiety
grew. I could not keep the palms of my hands dry. A small,
steady tremor ran through my stomach. I felt as if I would
explode—or more correctly *implode,* swallow myself up until I
vanished completely. I sat in the bar and rehearsed what I
would say when I finally saw him, what cool but loving expression I would wear on my face.

And then Javier was walking toward me, his eyes red and
swollen, his shoulders hunched, his legs stiff as an arthritic's. And
then I ran to him, crying, and wrapped my arms around his
wide chest and pulled him close and said: *Javier Javier Javier.* And
then I felt a sudden, terrifying sensation that I was embracing

a new corpse, a familiar shell from which the life had just been emptied.

ME: Did you know that when you stepped off the plane that day, your wife knew you had never really returned from Argentina?

JAVIER: What does this mean? Of course I returned! I am here!

ME: No, Javier. Your wife knew only your body had returned on the plane. She knew that your heart and mind were still thousands of miles away in Argentina.

JAVIER: (Like winter.) My wife always believes she knows more than she really does.

ME: Actually, your wife knows more than she really *says*. For example, did you know that yesterday your wife sorted through the negatives to the photographs you brought back from Argentina?

JAVIER: (Silence.)

ME: Did you know that when your wife compared the negatives to the photographs, she discovered five photographs missing?

JAVIER: (Silence. A slight blanching of the skin around the mouth.)

ME: Do you know which five photographs I am talking about?

JAVIER: I have no idea.

ME: But, Javier, those photographs are hidden in your passport. To have hidden them in your passport would have taken some calculated effort, correct? You must know which photographs I'm talking about.

JAVIER: I have no idea.

ME: Then let me describe them to you: There are, as I said, five. And in each one is the same woman. The woman is very young and very beautiful. My estimation is that she is about twenty or twenty-one. About your age. In one photograph you are holding this young woman very close to your body and smiling a very big smile. In another photograph you are kissing this young woman very passionately. In another photograph this young woman is sleeping in the tent I bought you for your birthday, and she is wearing nothing. The other two are simply portraits of her, yet there is a look in her eyes that is not without desire. Any viewer of these portraits would know that the young woman is on intimate terms with the photographer. The photographer, who is you.

JAVIER: I did not make love to her.

ME: Please answer the questions as they are asked. Did you make love to her?

JAVIER: No.

ME: Is there a possibility that you are *in* love with her?

JAVIER: No, there is no possibility.

ME: Is she perhaps the reason you are no longer certain of how you love your wife?

JAVIER: No.

ME: If the photographs are without meaning, if you did not make love to this woman, if you are not in love with this woman, then why did you hide the photographs?

JAVIER: Because I knew you would be angry if you saw them.

ME: (Sweetly.) Don't be ridiculous. I would not be angry. I am only a reporter. You mean to say that *your wife* would be angry.

JAVIER: Yes, my wife would be angry.

ME: And do you think your wife would have a reason to be angry if she saw the photographs?

JAVIER: No. I did nothing wrong.

ME: Then why did you hide the photographs?

JAVIER: I have already told you. I will not answer the same question two time.

ME: *Times.* With an S.

JAVIER: Times. But I will tell you this: My wife has not trusted me since the day we met.

ME: That is absolutely not true!

I stopped trusting Javier the day I realized I was in love with him. The day I realized I was in love with him was the day I realized I did not want to lose him.

This is how my mind works:

I   I AM IN LOVE WITH JAVIER
    A   Being in love with Javier makes me happy.
    B   I like being happy and want to be happy for as long as possible.
    C   If I lose Javier, I will no longer be happy.
    D   I do not want to lose Javier.

II REASONS I COULD LOSE JAVIER
    A   He could die. (Romantic but morbid.)
    B   He could return to Argentina to help support his family. (But I could go with him, couldn't I?)
    C   He could decide he no longer enjoys being with me:
        1   In this case, deciding he would rather be alone.
        2   In this case, deciding he would rather be with other women.
        3   In this case, *because* he has just been with another woman and thinks there is no comparison.

III WHO ARE THESE OTHER WOMEN?
    A   Younger.
    B   More beautiful.
    C   More beautiful because they are younger.

IV THERE WILL ALWAYS BE YOUNGER WOMEN

V   WHAT CAN I DO ABOUT LOSING JAVIER TO A YOUNGER WOMAN?
    A   Nothing.

    CONCLUSION
        Never trust Javier again.

ME: Javier, have you ever lied to your wife?
JAVIER: Never.
ME: Do you understand that your wife understands that this answer you just gave may be a lie? And if that is the case, then you have lied to your wife before.

JAVIER: Yes. I understand this.

ME: So actually, my asking you if you have ever lied to your wife was a fruitless question.

JAVIER: What is fruitless?

ME: Producing nothing beneficial—in this case, an answer.

JAVIER: So why did you ask the question?

ME: Because when you lie, Javier, your voice is always too sure of itself. Your face becomes slightly distorted as if you were doing a difficult exercise in mathematics. Like now.

JAVIER: Why are you doing this to me?

ME: I'm not doing anything to you. This is an interview, to which you agreed. I am only asking questions and you are only answering them—with or without the truth.

JAVIER: I can stop the interview at any time I want.

ME: Yes, but that would be ridiculous, wouldn't it? This is a perfect opportunity to tell an objective reporter what you do not have the courage to tell your wife. This is a perfect opportunity to say you will be leaving her.

JAVIER: (Silence. The face grows morose but the body relaxes.)

How long have I prepared for this moment? Possibly, one year. Possibly, since the day Javier and I took the bus downtown to pick up our marriage license. I was nervous, slightly giddy. I tried to seem calm, but my voice rose an octave higher and I laughed too much. Javier was very calm. Too calm. He looked as if he were on his way to buy a pair of shoes.

I asked: *Javier, aren't you just a little excited?*

And Javier said: *No. Why should I be excited?*

And I asked: *A little frightened?*

And Javier said: *No. Why should I be frightened?*

And I said: *People do not get married every day. What we are doing we will not do every day.*

And Javier said: *What we are doing is making our lives more convenience.*

And I said: *Convenient.*

And Javier said: *Convenient. I thought we had talked about this completely. I thought there was no doubt that marriage is not important.*

And I said: *Yes, but when you have been raised your whole life to believe otherwise, it's hard to dismiss that feeling of importance.*

And Javier said: *It's like I told you before: You take marriage too seriously.*

And I said: *No, in my mind I understand that I can never promise to love someone for the rest of my life, to be faithful to him forever.*

And Javier said: *In your mind, yes. But in your heart I think it is different. There is still time to change your mind, you know.*

And I said: *Let's drop the subject.*

And Javier said: *Okay.*

And I said: *You don't believe a person can love another person forever, do you?*

And Javier said: *Another person, maybe. But I cannot.*

ME: Where will you go from here?

JAVIER: Back to Argentina.

ME: (Not nausea exactly, but a sickness as if each cell of my body were slowly turning in on itself.) When?

JAVIER: I don't know. As soon as I have enough money for the ticket.

ME: How long will that take?

JAVIER: I don't know.

ME: But you must have some idea.

JAVIER: I said I don't know.

ME: An estimate. That's all I want.

JAVIER: Why? It doesn't matter.

ME: It matters.

JAVIER: Okay. A month, maybe. Maybe two.

ME: (Spit the word.) Fine.

JAVIER: You hate me, don't you?

ME: No. I am only a reporter. Your wife hates you.

———

Picture this:

A quiet Sunday afternoon in early summer, the light coming through the trees as if they are under water, and you are the drowned looking through the leaves at the light, knowing you have drowned by the strange way the trees are moving in the water's current. *The whole world has drowned . . .*

But this is only a metaphor for pain.

Actually, you are sitting on a roof fifty-plus feet in the air and the sun is going down and because of this the light is gold, really gold, and it swaddles your husband's face and chest and arms and legs, and you think he has never looked more beautiful. Then you look down at your own body, hoping there is some final justice in this world. And, yes, the light is also touching you, but it isn't the same. And your husband only stares out across the top of the city and sighs.

ME: Don't leave me, Javier.

JAVIER: But you are just a reporter. When the interview is over, I will leave you.

ME: You know what I mean. Don't leave me.

JAVIER: (Eyes averted.) You are just a reporter.

ME: (Hand grabbing his stubbled chin.) *Look at me!* I'm the woman you have lived with for over a year! I'm the woman you have made love with more times than you can name! I'm the woman who waited five weeks for you to come home and who felt so much loneliness she thought she would die! I'm not just a reporter, comprendes? I am your wife, Javier. No matter what you say, you married me and I am your wife!

JAVIER: I married a woman who took marriage too seriously.

ME: Then fuck the marriage!

JAVIER: (Smiling. What is it—callousness, or his own twisted pain?) Yes, I think that is what we will do, isn't it?

ME: And fuck you, too!

JAVIER: (Silence.)

ME: (Silence.)
JAVIER: (Silence.)
ME: (Silence.)
JAVIER: Look, the tape is finished. The interview is over.
ME: The tape was finished a long time ago.
JAVIER: Why didn't you tell me? A reporter has an obligation
         to say when the interview is over.
ME: (Suddenly very tired.) Stop it, Javier. Okay, okay, the
         interview is over. I'm not a reporter anymore.
JAVIER: (Standing.) Good. The interview is over.
ME: Yes, it's over. And where the hell do you think you're
         going?
JAVIER: The interview is over so I am leaving.

FOR THE RECORD:
     TIME: 8:00 P.M., one year ago.
     PLACE: The back steps of an old three-story mansion. (The
bodies damp and fragrant, the feet tangled on the ground.)
     Javier said: *This is my favorite moment of the day. What do you
call it?*
     And I said: *Evening.*
     And Javier said: *No, that is not it exactly. There is another word,
more specific.*
     And I said: *Twilight?*
     And Javier said: *Sure. That is a good word. Twilight. The time
seems not to move at twilight.*
     And I said: *But it is moving.*
     And Javier said: *Sure. It is moving.*

ME: Don't leave me, Javier.
JAVIER: (Calling.) I am leaving!
ME: How will I get down from the roof?
JAVIER: (Calling, with certainty.) You will find a ways.
ME: (To whom—Javier? No, I think not.) Find a *way*, damn
         it! Without the S! Without the goddamn S.

Blind

SHE SITS at the small scarred desk pushed against the window where, outside, it rains. Not heavily. Not lightly. Just a persistent, steady falling of water from the gray sky, with no wind and no terrible darkness and no strange olive light coming over the buildings as if the rain were about to cease.

The rain will not cease.

Her pale face like stone hovers inches above the notebook in which she writes. The bones are hard and angular, and the flesh is tight on the bones, caving in beneath the cheeks, at the temples, and around the eyes narrowed to thin slits—two dashes framing the bridge of her nose—a phrase empty of words, silent, and therefore more profound, like an unwritten sigh.

She is myopic. When she sets down the pen and looks up and out the window into the rain, she sees nothing but the deep green of the fuchsia bush (the pink blossoms fell with the first storms), the broad pastel facades of the buildings across the street, and the gray wet sky. She sees color and vague forms defined by color. There are no lines, no sharp edges to anything. Just one hue bleeding into the next, flatly, like a painting.

Years ago someone told her the Impressionists were myopic, painting the world precisely as they saw it: color and light. Color, of course, defined by light, the way an object reflects or absorbs luminescence from either the sun, naturally, or from the "false" light of a lamp or flame. Color without boundaries, without the sure geometry that makes it easy to point and say *tree* or *woman* quickly, certainly.

Half-blind and refusing now the devices that will make her vision clearer, she cannot name anything quickly except what she knows by its proximity to something else. And then it is not really her vision which assures her of its name but rather memory, and from memory, a rapid deduction:

There is a boulevard, and along the boulevard something large and straight rises from the pavement's edge, black on the bottom and green on top . . . green and floating like a verdant cloud, swaying a bit, not quite solid, the whiteness of sky breaking through in shimmering flecks. What else along a boulevard, and so tall and green and trembling, but a tree? What else!

But it is never that way exactly. There is never a reason to define one object at a time. No, that is not the way it happens. Nor is it the way her mind works in a world where each object is relevant to everything else and where she has lived long enough with such limited vision to put the objects together unconsciously. Although if someone were to ask—*But who would ask?*—she might have to pause for a moment, become quite certain before saying: "Why it's a tree, of course!"

She once told a lover (a sculptor, arrogant, not as wise as she'd first believed, nor as kind) about the theory of myopic Impressionists.

He laughed. "Absurd! The Impressionists went blind afterward, because of the way they painted, their precise techniques, the strain of breaking down each color into its primary components. Monet's concept of the envelope, for example. Painting not the object his eyes saw, but what came between his eyes and the object, what was enveloped between: atmosphere! The mere attempt of such an effort, *the mere attempt,* caused his eyes to go bad. Afterward, damn it! *Afterward* the Impressionists went blind!"

Although she thought it might have been pleasant to know the real truth—blinded before or after, or never really blind at all, just another romantic rumor that made an interesting history more interesting, more *colorful,* ha ha—in the end none of it really mattered. The paintings were made and then sold and then hung on walls, becoming yet another object added to the world's warehouse of objects. What difference did it make how they were conceived? Years passed. In the end, as in so many instances, the paintings became more famous than the painters. Men and women and even children (she remembers what she knew and did not know as a child) who had never heard the name Monet, or had heard it once and then forgotten it, not considering it worthwhile to remember . . . men and women and even children recognized, say, Monet's *Water Lilies* and perhaps even liked the paintings. But what did they care of the man who painted them? The man sitting for hours beside a lily pond, pulling from its surface not the real vision of lilies but the *impression* of them and consequently going blind?

Yes. In the end, more often than not, it was the painting that was remembered and adored, as if it were wholly responsible for its own creation, godlike, reaching back into its own history and moving itself forward into its future. Yes, that's right. And not only paintings. Even the few artists who were known to the pedestrian crowd. Picasso, for example.

For example, who remembers Picasso's parents? Or thinks of them much? And who wonders where they were when they conceived their prodigious son, or how they made love: happily, in an amorous atmosphere of candlelight and wine and the sweet smell of new grass coming through the window that evening, or morning? Or among that sweet new grass? Or in a fit of rage—Picasso's father taking Picasso's mother with a violence that had nothing to do with love, and she submitting to his frenzied strength, weeping, despising him and her own pitiful life, already hefting the bulk of her hope and passion onto the unborn child?

What difference does it make now? Picasso is dead. Even when he was alive, who remembered his parents?

The rain falls.

She cannot see the rain or hear it from within the darkening room, yet she knows it is there: the dampness within her bones. The heaviness of the season like a cold stone inside her belly. The season only now beginning and so far to go before the jasmine blooms again, before the sun swings higher in the afternoon sky, before the breezes become light and dry and sweetened with the fragrance of the sea.

Too far to go, she thinks, *and so not worth the wait or the longing.*

Ah, the longing!

Once I longed to embrace a man so completely I would pull his entire being inside the cavern of my breasts, and pull him closer still, past that soft full flesh, past the jail of my ribs, past the warm sweet heart-blood, locking him inside the house of my soul.

Embrace him! Possess him! Let him be the glorious spirit who possessed me!

And me, content, so warmed by his presence that no wind could ever chill me. Nor death.

She sighs. As she does, a gust of wind rushes through the wet leaves of the fuchsia, sighing too. The rain bends momentarily south, blowing against the window. She hears it. Leaning closer to the pane, she sees the rivulets.

She whispers, "Rain."

The wind stops. The rivulets slowly drain and vanish.

She places the palm of each hand over her eyes and looks at the darkness there.

When she was a child, she shut herself inside a closet and stuffed a blanket into the slit of light beneath the door. Darkness surrounded her. The kind of darkness that cannot be penetrated, in

which everything—even the whiteness of a hand—disappears.
She opened her eyes wide and still saw nothing.

Her mother called and called to her.

The closet was warm. She lay down, drawing her knees up
to her chest, and fell asleep. When she woke and stepped out of
the closet it was as if she had given birth to herself.

So who, besides she, will remember her mother? Will wonder why her mother called and called to her that day, so softly,
flutelike—the day her father died—and then stopped calling,
tired and choked on her own sorrow?

Who will remember? Who will know?

Even knowing, who would care?

She removes her hands and opens her eyes. Nothing has changed.
There is no rebirth.

She takes a sip of tea, which has grown cold, then stands.
How tall she feels! How tight the room around her seems! The
ceiling too low, the walls too close. Yet isn't it simply because
she cannot discern distance or depth, blind as she is?

A week ago the room was large. She danced through it in
the morning, easily as a nymph. Her body seemed unbound by
gravity, floating, deliriously light. She held her naked arms in
front of her and noted their thin elegant beauty, turning them
slowly in the air like an exotic dancer, watching the muscles
convulse and relax, convulse and relax. Then she lay down on
the bed and stretched her arms up toward the ceiling, her
shoulders tense, her hands loose and poised it seemed on the
edge of an embrace. And in the wide gulf between her arms she
imagined him, her last lover, sprawled upon the valley she had
built around him, and he moving slowly against the terrain of
that valley, then moving inside it. Oh, it was a fine dream! She
smiled and closed her eyes and pressed her hands upward into
the air, and a throbbing began between her thighs. That singular deep hungry throbbing, the antithesis of pain. Something to
lean toward rather than retreat from.

She lets the weight of her body fall onto the bed, thinks once about raising her arms toward the ceiling. Thinks twice. Changes her mind. Her arms with their loose hands fall over her chest in a blank gesture of resignation. They hold nothing and no one—not even, it seems, her own cold body.

And so there is no reason to lie down: She is not tired and there is no comfort in a cold bed that is just a bed because there is no life in it to make it otherwise.

Her bed: functional. A practical mass of wire and cotton and steel and wood which carries her body through sleep.

When her husband (the only husband she ever had) came to live with her before their marriage, he was poor and she was poor and they did not even own a bed. At night they spread a tattered quilt on the wooden floor and slept there: arms and legs locked together, faces so close it was impossible to know whose warm breath they felt on their cheeks—their own or the other's. And the floor was so hard, so cold! Their bones shifted against the wood during sleep. When they woke in the morn-ing their skin would be discolored, bruised—deep red circles that eventually turned blue and then faded to a yellow-green.

Where was the pain then?

She would throw the blanket off her body and point to a hip or knee or elbow and say, "Look!"

Her husband would place a single finger on the redness there and coo, "My poor Ceci! Oh, my poor, poor Ceci!"

Yet where was the pain?

Compassionate, her husband feigned sickness and did not eat for a week and sold his old leather coat, the only coat he owned, and took the money he saved from not eating and the money he received from selling the coat and bought a small used bed: narrow, sized for a child, with a weak spring frame and a tufted mattress that sagged in the middle so that when they slept they could not help but lay pressed tightly against each other, no matter which way they turned in their dreams.

But that was in the beginning. When they loved each other. When sleeping side by side was all they wanted to do. Later, when they had more money and a bigger bed—when they had everything that did not really matter and had lost the one thing that did, when they had so much more and so much less—they rarely slept with their bodies pressed tightly together and therefore knew, later, that it was good they had loved each other so much when there was no bed and when the bed was old and narrow and sagging in the middle.

She stands in the center of the room and looks at her bed. She knows there are roses on the coverlet though she cannot see them clearly. What she sees are patches of red bleeding across a dull white plain, like watercolor spilled on wet paper and then left to dry, like stifled weeping amid silence.

Yet she knows they are roses. Her blindness does not make them less than what they are. The fact that she cannot see the world as clearly as it was created does not make it something other than what it already is.

And what is the world, anyway, but an illusion of convenience?

Once, in the year before her brother died, he pointed to a cypress tree and squealed, "Look! A tree made of rock!" She was two years younger and adored him and thus believed everything he said. Besides, the tree *did* appear solid as stone: an immutable monolith rising out of the soil as if the earth's leisurely shifting had exposed it to the world.

He picked up a rock and threw it into the thicket of cypress needles. Four white birds flew out, lamenting—*Or were they rejoicing: freed from a life inside stone?*—lamenting as they scattered in four directions, regrouped and headed toward the sea.

Even her brother was startled, amazed. Her brother: older, wiser, but just a child, really. Eight years old. She spent the next and final year of his life throwing rocks at stones, hoping to release the birds imprisoned there inside.

———

This realization—*The world, illusory as it is, will be no more and no less when I am absent from it*—grips her around the throat and for a moment she can neither swallow nor breathe nor open her mouth to imitate breathing.

Panic!

So much panic that her mind grinds to an entropic halt and she remains standing paralyzed between one thought and the next.

Eventually her marriage grew intolerable. There were no quarrels, no accusations, no slamming doors. Only silence. A silence so immense she felt less significant than a mote on the skin of the earth.

One day she could neither swallow nor breathe nor open her mouth to imitate breathing. She got in her car and drove without destination, meandering through the streets of her neighborhood, then the streets of more distant neighborhoods.

It was autumn. Leaves covered the lawns. Acorns and walnuts and pecans fell from branches and bounced in the damp leaf-strewn grass, rolled along sidewalks, accumulated in gutters.

Halfway down a sunlit street, a squirrel carrying a large walnut ran in front of her car and stopped and turned and stared at the tires rolling toward it. It started to retreat the way it had come, then changed its mind and headed across the street again, then retreated, then moved forward. She lifted her foot from the accelerator to give the animal time to choose a path. The vehicle drew nearer. The squirrel froze before the left front tire. She slammed on her brakes, but it was too late. She pinched her eyes shut against the tiny *bump* and *thud*.

The sun gleamed, unobstructed. Birds sang in the branches of trees. A large walnut rolled quietly down the middle of the street.

She shut off the engine and for the first time in years wept uncontrollably. When there were no more tears, she drove home and walked into the kitchen where her husband sat reading a newspaper and laid a large walnut in front of him and said, "I'm leaving you."

Move!

She sets her feet in motion without knowing where she will go, turning in circles before determining a straight path. She goes to the bathroom and sits on the toilet and waits. Her bowels are empty, her bladder is empty. She wipes her dry bottom, stands, goes to the sink. She turns on the faucet, washes her hands and dries them on the flannel of her nightgown. She lifts her head. She does not wish to look at her face in the mirror yet she cannot help herself: an old vain habit.

From three feet away her face appears as nothing but a moon framed by the whitening cloud of her hair. From three feet away even her eyes—gray and lashless—are too pale to appear as something distinct and separate, something more than fading scars on a cold surface, no longer lit from within.

When did the light go out?

And what caused that internal light in the first place—love, hope, simple youth? Is youth simpler than old age? No. Less wise, perhaps, but not simpler. It is the simplicity of old age, in fact, that makes it dull. Intolerably, unbearably, unceremoniously dull.

She opens her mouth slowly, stretching it until her lips feel as if they will tear.

There it is: Black hole. Hollow. Void.

Of all her lovers, M was the best. (Or was she at her best when she loved him?) A poet who did not bother putting his poems to paper. Who believed the sight of the eyes interfered with the vision of the soul.

She asked, "Am I beautiful?"

He closed his eyes, pressed an ear to her chest and concentrated hard before replying, "Yes. Very beautiful."

"You are beautiful, too," she said.

His face drawn in sadness: "Please don't say that while looking at me. Please don't say that with your eyes open."

She turned her head and looked out the window into the
darkness. "You are," she said confidently, "beautiful, too."

He smiled, laid one hand on her forehead, the other on her
chin and opened her mouth gently, wide. He put his lips inside
the hollow he had made and filled it with words:

Here is my soul in the shape of my tongue.

Here is my heart in the shape of my voice.

Here are my fingers in the shape of my teeth . . .

When she inhaled, his words carved themselves on the wall
of her life.

People die. The circumstances of their deaths do not always
match the import of their lives.

One morning M stepped into a bathtub of running water
and slipped and fell backward onto the floor. His head struck
the porcelain rim of the toilet and he died—not instantly: legs
dangling half-submerged in the bathtub, arms flung wide as if
reaching toward an embrace, head settled hard against the cold
base of the toilet, mouth agape, nose running, eyes open and
staring at the overhead light in surprise.

She found the body. After her horror had dissipated, she
knelt down beside him. She cradled his penis—surprisingly
erect—pressed her lips to his still bleeding ear and whispered,
"What did you see, the moment death came for you? Was it
beautiful? Did it make you think of me?"

She closes her mouth. The hollow is filled. No, not filled.
Disguised. It still exists within, a vast thing: tangible, heavy,
omnivorous. Feeding on memories that leap, claws sprung, out
of the past.

So many lovers—*What were their names?*—and all dead now.
Dead or lost among the ashes of living. That gray place into
which acquaintances disappear when they walk out of one's life

forever. Impossible to see them precisely as they were—fallacies intact—rather they exist as ghosts caught in the periphery of the mind's eye: either good, or bad, depending on the circumstances of their departure.

No, they were all good. It's just that, sometimes, their lives got in the way of their goodness.

K, for example:
"Here. I've got a gift for you." His smile like that of an over-anxious child.

"It's expensive."

"Sure, baby. The stones are real. The gold's high carat."

"It's stolen."

Now the child becomes the man, the anger proportionate to the change. "Can't you even say thank you? Can't you even show some goddamn appreciation?"

"The things you steal get bigger and more expensive. I'm just afraid that someday . . ."

"I'm trying to tell you I love you! Shit! Can't you even *acknowledge* that?"

She acknowledged that. She removed her eyeglasses smudged with tears, and as she leaned forward to kiss him, blindly, she caught sight of Death grinning just behind his left shoulder.

Poor K! Boy, man, lover, thief. One bullet through the pelvis, one through the chest, one through the hollow beneath his left eye.

So many dead, now. Or lost among the ashes.

Three days ago her last lover (a man she had slept with for eight months, whom she had never loved) put his hat on and said, "I'm leaving you."

She nodded, pursed her lips, touched her hair as if a moth had suddenly settled upon it. She said, "I should collect your things."

There wasn't much: a toothbrush, a razor, a single sock.

"I'm sorry, I don't know where the other one . . ." Her voice trailed off.

"Don't apologize," he said harshly, as if it were his final lesson to her. He took his things and opened the door and walked out—past the fuchsia still in bloom, down the sidewalk, to the front steps where he briefly turned and looked at her standing in the doorway, and then continued onward, away.

It was his final look that terrified her. A look of pity and condolence, even disgust. A look that made her realize, too suddenly and without warning, that the delusion was over: She was no longer young, no longer beautiful, and thus no longer able to convince herself that she was young and beautiful.

Youth and beauty: The only two things of value she believes she possessed.

Perhaps if she'd had an occupation—*What was I ever good at besides seduction? Really! What else could I have done?*—perhaps owned a passion beyond men and their passions, and the vanity men and their passions fed in her. A talent, a skill, a competence that burgeoning time would have fortified, not demolished. Even love.

If I'd at least been good at love.

She searches for the sock: behind the couch, under the bed, inside closets and drawers. What she finds instead is dust: her own dead skin accumulating around her, thick as bone ash and pain.

So much dust, so much dying!

She looks around and makes a rapid deduction: There is as much of her dead in the house as there is of her alive and breathing.

Am I still breathing?

She bends toward the mantle and exhales through her nostrils; her breath chases the dust from the wood. It floats awhile in the air, then falls. She thrusts a hand out to let the dust settle upon her skin.

What will become of the things I know, the things I've seen?

Her eyes fill with tears, and for a moment she can see quite clearly the rain falling upon the fuchsia, green leaves shivering from the water's weight, branches black and slick and dripping. A last blossom—stubborn or late blooming—finally releases its hold and falls among the others cluttering the ground.

Though I would like to love again, I know I will not.

How do I know?

One knows.

As she turns from the window (loneliness piercing her heart with its knife's edge of inevitability) she spies a single sock in the corner among the dust and damp and dark.

This is it: the end of things. The end.

Do not let it endure longer than the beginning.

Outside, it rains—not heavily, not lightly, just a persistent steady falling of water from the gray sky, with no wind and no terrible darkness and no strange olive light coming over the buildings as if the rain were about to cease.

She bends down, her bones snapping like damp firewood, and picks up the final blossom and brings it to her face and peers inside at its blood-red heart. She smells it, presses it against her eyelids one at a time, then to her lips which she opens, laying the blossom on her tongue.

Although it would have been pleasant to know the truth—blinded before or after, or never really blind at all—in the end, none of it matters.

She closes her eyes and looks at the darkness there. She closes her mouth and swallows.

I Am Telling You Lies

ESTEBAN WAS A LIAR. We all knew it, yet we loved him anyway.

My sister Diedre loved him because he once sent her a dozen roses and told her she was beautiful. No one had ever told Diedre she was beautiful before because, by American standards, she wasn't. Diedre was fat, her nose was too big for her small eyes and thin lips, and her white face and shoulders were scarred by acne. The scars were purple and round and reminded me of tiny pressed flowers. Even now when I remember Diedre as she was then, I think of dried violets pressed between the pages of a perfect blank book.

Jorge, my first husband, loved Esteban because Esteban was the first South American he met when he came to the United States. Jorge thought this was significant. But Jorge thought everything was significant. He thought there was a reason for everything and that you had to suspend even the most ordinary moments until you discovered why they occurred. Jorge believed in God. Personally, I think you can hang onto things for years and they still don't make any sense.

I loved Esteban *because* he lied. This disgusted Diedre and Jorge. Diedre and Jorge believed lying to be wrong at all times. I think sometimes it's okay if it doesn't hurt anyone. Esteban's lies were harmless. Not once did we cry because of Esteban's lies. Usually we smiled. (Diedre and Jorge smiled secretly because they knew that to smile openly was to tell the world lying is okay.) Esteban's lies didn't even hurt Esteban, and if Diedre and Jorge were here right now I think they would have a hard time arguing with that. In fact, Esteban's lies were what made him interesting. Without them, he would have been a very dull person.

Jorge had been in the United States only two weeks when he met Esteban. Jorge's English was terrible then. He knew how to say where he was from, how to ask directions to the bathroom, and how to order a beer. That was about it. One night he met a girl in a bar who spoke a little Spanish, so they got drunk together. The girl took him home with her and they made love.

The next morning Esteban arrived at her apartment with a bouquet of white lilies and an anxious smile. Although he had not yet even kissed the girl, he had brought her many gifts and she had accepted them, and thus he had foolishly concluded that something magical had passed between them. When Esteban found Jorge and the girl in bed together he was very angry, until he discovered that Jorge was from Argentina. Likewise, Jorge was very nervous, until he discovered that Esteban was from Bolivia. (I think South Americans love other South Americans when they are in the United States and in the beginning will forgive each other almost anything.) Esteban and Jorge embraced one another and sat on the bed and talked for three hours.

The girl was happy about this sudden friendship, and relieved, until Esteban and Jorge said they were going out for lunch and would not be back—ever. Then she became furious and threw a heavy glass at them as they were walking out the door. Esteban ducked. Jorge didn't. The day I met Jorge, he'd just had five stitches removed from his forehead.

Women loved Jorge. I imagine they still do. (He was dark and beautiful. He had strong white teeth that he liked to show to the world. His teeth were like amulets: when he revealed them, women became soft and complaisant no matter what irremissible deed he had done.) But when I met him, women loved him more. His English was so bad it made everyone smile. And because he understood so little of what was being said around him, he always wore an expression of utter desperation.

I think women love desperate men. I think desperate men make women feel powerful and worthy all at once. It is a woman's instinct to protect and nurture babies, small animals, and desperate men. Jorge knew this. So even when his English became better and he felt comfortable in his new country, he continued to appear desperate. He would say, "Please, I don't speak English." And the women would smile and take him home and feed him and make love to him, and in the morning when he left and never came back, the women didn't mind so much because they felt they had done something very good for one of the world's desperate men.

It was the same with me except Jorge came back, and he kept coming back until he stayed. At least for a while.

I don't know why I thought Esteban would be tall and handsome. When Jorge spoke of him, I imagined a giant with strong bones and a serious face. But Esteban was short and comical looking. He had a thin wide mouth like a snake's, and eyes like a hungry weasel's. When he smiled his nose spread halfway across his face. His skin was dark yellow as if he suffered from liver disease. He was very skinny. When I met him, he embraced me and I embraced him and I thought I would break every bone in his body.

"Well, then, hello, Tamara," said Esteban. (He spoke in staccato, saying *Ta-ma-ra* as if tapping out a cadence on a snare drum.) "You are as beautiful as I imagined, and much taller." He kissed my hand.

"You're shorter," I said, "and not what I imagined at all."

Esteban sighed. "That, I am sure, is most painfully true."

"I'm sorry. I didn't mean that the way it sounded."

"No, that is exactly the way you meant it," he said cheer-
fully. "That is why you are embarrassed now. Speaking the truth
is a huge responsibility. But Jorge has told me you have a good
heart, so I forgive you."

I looked at Jorge. Jorge grinned at me as if to say, "See? Isn't
Esteban as wonderful as I claimed?" I shrugged my shoulders
and sat down.

Esteban sat on the arm of the couch. His thin legs bounced
quickly up and down on the balls of his feet. (Esteban was a
nervous person. Only dead could he have remained motionless
for more than a minute.) Jorge, who was still grinning like a fed
cat, positioned himself on the other side of the room where he
could see both Esteban and me. He had a look of great anticipation, as if he expected something magnificent to happen.

"So, Esteban," I said, "Jorge tells me you studied in the Soviet
Union."

"This is true," said Esteban. "I studied in Russia for two
years. It was beautiful."

"Why did you choose Russia to study agriculture?"

Esteban looked puzzled.

"It was agriculture you studied, wasn't it?"

"No," said Esteban, coughing a bit, "mathematics. The same
as I am studying here in America."

I looked accusingly at Jorge. Jorge looked accusingly at Esteban, then began speaking very rapidly to him in Spanish.
Esteban responded very rapidly in Spanish. This went on for
a long time. Their voices grew louder. I understood nothing
except that Jorge was very angry. (Anger does not need a trans-
lator.)

After they had quieted down, Jorge was still frowning a little, but Esteban turned to me and smiled.

"I studied agriculture in Bolivia," he said, "nct Russia. And
for one year only. My father owns a very big plantation, you
see. Very big. He wanted me to study agriculture and business
so I could operate the plantation when he became too old. My

father has sixty-one years and is not strong. But I did not like agriculture. I did not like the plantation. On the plantation my father works Indians whom he pays almost nothing. They work very hard from very early in the morning to very late at night. They live like dogs. I don't like the plantation because it is a place of slavery."

Jorge, who did not like injustice, said, "Que horrible!"

Esteban nodded grimly.

I said, "But if you controlled the plantation, you could change things, right? You could pay the workers better wages and make them work fewer hours, right?"

"That is possible," said Esteban. Then he shook his head. "But it would not be so simple as that. Everywhere in Bolivia the plantation workers have lived like dogs for many years. They do not question it because it is all that they know."

"Or because they are afraid to question," offered Jorge.

Esteban ignored him. "If I gave my workers more money and shorter hours, news of this would travel fast. Every worker in Bolivia would want to come to my plantation. And when I had no work to give them, they would return to their plantations and demand more money and fewer hours. Perhaps there would be a revolution. The other plantation owners would hate me. Probably they would have me killed."

He thought about this a moment and smiled. "Yes. They would certainly have me killed. They would hang me by my neck from a very tall tree, but every other moment they would raise me up to make sure I did not die immediately. Then they would cut off my toes, one by one, with a rusty knife. Then they would cut off my fingers, one by one. Then they would cut out my eyes and my tongue. Then they would cut off . . ." he stood and raised one arm in the air as if holding a knife, then he let it fall in front of him, making a whooshing sound with his mouth as the arm passed in front of his zipper, ". . . my huevos!"

And he laughed.

"That is crazy," said Jorge, but I could see he was amused.

Esteban sat down again and immediately sobered. "Yes, crazy, my friend. But true, of course. These men who have much money love their money and will do anything to keep it."

"What about your father?" I asked. "Does he love his money, too?"

"Sure," said Esteban with nonchalance. "My father would be the first to cut off my huevos if I were to change the ways of his plantation. But he would do it more slowly, centimeter by centimeter. Then he would take the pieces of my flesh and toss them to the birds and dance and sing while I disappeared into —como se dice?—gullets."

"I don't believe you," said Jorge.

And Esteban opened wide his hungry-weasel eyes and said, "But I swear it is the truth!"

Diedre liked Esteban immediately. When they were introduced, Esteban walked right up and kissed her on both cheeks as if her purple scars did not exist. Diedre blushed and the scars grew darker. At twenty-seven she was still painfully shy. She lived in fear of people laughing at her big nose or fat stomach or purple scars. Yet when someone paid her a compliment, she grew dizzy with embarrassment. To Diedre, compliments were like foreign words; she did not know how to translate them. She could have counted each and every compliment she'd ever received on one plump hand.

"It's a pleasure to meet you," said Diedre like a new queen, and I thought she would bend her knees in a curtsy.

"Ah, Diedre," said Esteban, pronouncing her name *Dee-AY-dray,* as if he were still in Bolivia. "You are as beautiful as I imagined and much . . . ah . . . taller." He kissed her hand.

Jorge poked an elbow into my ribs and gave a little cough.

"Thank you," said Diedre, blushing. "Please, everyone have a seat. I'll get some wine." She walked to the kitchen, and we could hear her stockings rubbing together at her thighs. (Fat women, I have since concluded, always move with a whisper.)

"You have a very nice house," Esteban called after her, raising his eyebrows and slowly nodding from left to right.

This was, in fact, quite true. Diedre's house was big for one person and tastefully, though not extravagantly, furnished. Most of her income went into the house. The rest went toward food and expensive chocolates and three or four new dresses each year. The dresses were only for the office. She had virtually no social life.

"Diedre is an accountant," I told Esteban. "She does very well for herself."

"An accountant!" said Esteban with a finger raised in the air as if testing the wind. "Such a coincidence! My sister is an accountant, also. She lives here, in America."

Jorge shifted in his chair. "I did not know you had a sister in the United States."

"Oh, yes," said Esteban. "She has been here for five, maybe six years. Her English is very good. Excellent. *No accent.* But I think that is because her husband is an actor."

I smiled.

Jorge cocked an eyebrow. "An actor?"

"Sure. He lives in Hollywood, in a incredible house with a swimming pool and tennis courts. Etcetera."

"What is his name?" asked Jorge.

Esteban paused and reached into his left shirt pocket for a cigarette. "Robert," he said. "Robert . . . Lincoln."

"Interesting," said Jorge, cocking his eyebrow higher, "but I have never heard of this Robert Lincoln. Is he in movies or in television?"

"Ah, movies, of course! Television is too . . . *insignificant* for Robert. In fact, Robert is an actor only in *Italian* cinema."

"But you said he lives in Hollywood," complained Jorge.

"Sure," said Esteban. "Of course. He lives in Hollywood, but he travels to Italy one time each year to act in a movie, then he returns home to Hollywood. You see, my sister the accountant works in Hollywood. She likes her job very much. If she did not like it, they would maybe live in Italy all year. Robert is very famous in Italy, you see. In Italy he is a very big star."

I smiled.

Jorge said, "Hm."

Diedre came whispering back into the room with a tray of glasses and bottle of wine. Watching her made me sigh: She was a nice girl. She did not swear or smoke or gossip. She drank alcohol only at meals or on special occasions, and then only wine. She was fat, she was saving herself for marriage, she prayed twice a day. She was so different from me we could have been strangers.

She set the tray in front of Esteban and poured one glass of wine and handed it to him with trembling fingers. "Es–Esteb-Es-Es–" she stammered.

"Esteban," said Esteban.

Diedre's scars grew darker. "I'm sorry. I don't speak Spanish."

"But of course not!" cried Esteban. He reached for the glass and let his fingers rest a moment on hers. "You are an American. You live in America. You have no need for Spanish."

Diedre, always grateful for small kindnesses, was grateful to Esteban. She sat near him and watched him closely, smiling like a monk. She forgot Jorge and I were in the room; we helped ourselves to a drink.

Esteban said, "This is muy lindo," and he rolled the wine around in his mouth. "Quite wonderful."

"I'm glad you like it," said Diedre. "I don't know very much about wine. I buy the ones that have interesting names, that sound exotic. Sometimes I get lucky. Other times not so lucky. I remember once I bought a burgundy that sounded French but wasn't, and I had diarrhea for a whole week!"

This last sentence slipped out of Diedre's mouth accidentally and her face burned and her scars glowed darkly. Diedre was not the type to talk about her bodily functions in the presence of strangers. She tried to smile but the effort transformed her mouth into a grimace. She bent over her shoes and pretended a sudden concern for invisible scuff marks. Watching Diedre's embarrassment was, for me, like watching a contestant make a fool of herself on a game show. But unlike the TV viewer, I could always save Diedre from humiliation. I'd had years of practice. Although nothing was ever said after these episodes, I knew Diedre was always grateful by the way she looked at me with watery eyes.

"Esteban's sister is an accountant, too," I said quickly. "He says she lives in Hollywood."

Diedre raised herself up again and the bright color slowly faded from her face. "Really?" she asked Esteban, then turned to me and smiled with watery eyes.

Esteban blew a smoke ring and lay back in his chair. "Yes. It's true. My sister is an accountant and she lives in Hollywood."

"What firm does she work for?" asked Diedre.

Esteban paused. "My sister does not work for a firm, exactly."

"Oh. Then who?"

Esteban studied the tip of his cigarette for a moment, then said, "Movie stars. My sister is a private accountant for movie stars."

And Jorge sarcastically mumbled, "But, of course."

Esteban believed Hollywood and everything associated with it was the epitome of the American Dream. This was odd since Esteban never went to movies. At least that's what he told us. He told us he did not like movies. He told us movies—especially American ones—were the bacteria behind the decadence spreading throughout the world.

"It is an epidemic," said Esteban one afternoon as he, Jorge, and I were having lunch together at the university cafeteria. "They show American movies everywhere, even in Bolivia. As a consequence, Bolivian girls become pregnant."

"Esteban, boludazo!" laughed Jorge. "It is not possible for girls in Bolivia to become pregnant from watching American movies. That is not smart biology, my friend." And Jorge laughed again.

Esteban frowned and tapped the filter of his unlit cigarette on the table. "You know that is not what I meant," he said quietly. "What I meant is that girls in Bolivia watch American movies. In American movies the girls are very—*liberated*. They make love with every man they meet. They take off their clothes for strangers. They dance naked on beaches and in nightclubs. Even if it is a movie about war, there are women jumping in and out of beds. So. Girls in Bolivia, who believe that to be an American girl is to be rich and lucky and fashionable, imitate what they see on the movie screen. But on the movie screen American girls do not often get pregnant, do they? No. In Bolivia, however, they do. And often after the very first intercourse. Bolivian girls are quite fertile, you see."

"Hollywood is not America," I told him.

"Ah," said Esteban, raising a finger and tipping it toward me. "But perhaps America is Hollywood."

Of course, this conversation occurred much later, long after Esteban had forgotten all about having a sister who was a Hollywood accountant.

Diedre, however, did not forget. Nor did she forget the ripening seed of thought Esteban had planted in her head during that first afternoon as he told her, "Perhaps you should consider moving to Hollywood, Diedre. You would do very well there." He swept his arm through the air. "You have done very well here, yes?"

"I've done okay," Diedre said with efficient modesty.

"In Hollywood," continued Esteban, "you could be a *very rich woman*. People would pay you much to take care of their money."

Diedre nodded. Her eyes got a faraway look in them. Even then I knew she was imagining her *very rich life* in Hollywood: a miraculous life, without a big nose or fat stomach or purple scars.

"Yes," continued Esteban. "The more money people have, the more they wish to hold onto it. It is the sickness of the world." He took a long drag on his cigarette. "Ah, but in Russia . . ."

———

Esteban spoke of Russia the way a passionate man speaks of a beautiful woman. There was not a single conversation which he did not manage to steer toward that geography.

By the time I met him, he had been away from the Soviet Union for almost two years. He told Jorge that the only reason he had left was because he had impregnated the daughter of a Soviet diplomat. He said the diplomat was going to have him publicly executed for his crime, so in order to save his life he had bribed a naval officer to stow him away on a battleship that was sailing from Leningrad to Warsaw, Poland. (Jorge had never learned world geography well enough to know that Warsaw is nearly two hundred miles inland from the Baltic Sea. And even if he had known, I do not think it would have mattered. He liked movies about spies and secret agents and incredibly lucky adventurers.)

Esteban told Diedre that the only reason he had left the Soviet Union was because of a broken heart. He told her that he had fallen deeply in love with a Catholic girl, a girl so pious and brave that on Christmas Eve she had carried a picture of the Virgin Mary to Red Square and tacked it over a poster of Lenin and knelt down before it and prayed out loud. The KGB, of course, had arrested her, and she had been shipped to Siberia where, Esteban was later informed, she had eventually died of consumption. (This story had made Diedre weep for days.)

One evening Esteban got very drunk and told me that the only reason he had left the Soviet Union was because the term of his scholarship had ended and his father had wished him to finish his education in the United States. I believe this story was true.

I could not know what Esteban's life was like in the Soviet Union, but I believe it was better than his life in the United States. At some point during his two-year stay there, Esteban had become a member of the Junior Communists League. That's what he said.

One night he invited Jorge, Diedre, and I to his apartment for drinks and showed us his Junior Communists League lapel pin. Jorge was impressed. Diedre was nervous. I was saddened. It was the way he held the pin in the center of his palm, the way his palm trembled as he held the pin toward us, making certain the yellow light of his one lamp illuminated the bright enamel completely. And it was the way Esteban himself looked at the pin in amazement, as if he could not believe it belonged to him, could not believe he had ever belonged to it (the League), could not believe the League or, for that matter, any important group had accepted him just as he was: without the lies he carried around like useful stones in his knapsack-of-a-heart. In all of Esteban's life, I do not believe such acceptance ever had been granted him. Not in Bolivia. And certainly not in the United States, where he was foreign and not handsome and not made of money and studied mathematics and was therefore considered repulsive and odd to most people he met. Nor do I believe he would ever be granted such acceptance again. I think Esteban did not believe so, either, and that is ultimately what I saw in his expression as he stared at the glowing pin of the Junior Communists League: a proud but utter disbelief in his own past, and a dreadful precognition of his lonely future. It saddened me.

Of course, just before Esteban showed us his pin, he pulled the shades and drew the curtains and locked the front door. He unplugged his telephone and carried it into the bathroom and set it on the bathroom sink. He ran water down an open drain and turned on an old transistor radio very loud, then stepped out, closing the bathroom door against the terrible noise. The ritual made me smile. Jorge rolled his eyes. Diedre began to perspire just above her thin lips.

"Necessary precautions," he whispered to us while removing the lapel pin from the tissue paper which enveloped it. "I believe I've told you before, the CIA has been following me since I left Russia. I recognized them immediately at the John F. Kennedy Airport, the moment I stepped from the plane. They always wear black sunglasses, you know, and unexciting gray suits. Also, on the train from New York to St. Louis, they sat in the compartment next to mine. And now, many times at night I hear them crawling in the bushes outside my window. I hear the static of their two-way radios."

Jorge squinted up at the ceiling, then looked at Esteban and frowned. "You took a bus from New York to St. Louis."

"No," said Esteban, "a train."

"You said to me a bus," Jorge insisted.

"You misunderstood."

"I did not misunderstand."

Jorge leaned forward, ready to debate the issue until dawn, but Esteban simply shrugged and turned his complete attention to unwrapping the tissue paper from around his Junior Communists League lapel pin.

Esteban wanted to live with Jorge and me. He never said this but I know it was true. He came to our apartment almost every day and would spend many hours talking with us and telling us fantastic stories. Sometimes we would have to yawn four or five times and look at our watches again and again, commenting on the late hour, before Esteban would finally rise to leave. On days when he was not at our apartment, he phoned. Sometimes he phoned three times in one day. Esteban told us more than once, "Jorge, Tamara, you have created a very comfortable life for yourselves in a world where comfort is not easily found." And he was right. In the beginning Jorge and I were very comfortable. We were young, we cared about the world, we were determined not to want more than we needed, and we had all that we needed and more: We had each other. In the beginning, at least, that was enough.

Esteban's life, on the other hand, was not so comfortable. He lived in a tiny studio apartment in the heart of a violent neighborhood. The apartment was cold in winter because Esteban would not set the thermostat above fifty-five degrees. In the summer the apartment was hot because there was no air conditioning and Esteban's small window fan only sucked the stifling outside air into the apartment and moved it thickly about the room. There were cockroaches year-round even though Esteban was a tidy person.

Although he did not own many things and owned nothing of real value, his apartment was burglarized twice. He claimed the robberies were not robberies at all but rather the CIA looking for evidence of conspiracy.

One evening after Jorge, Diedre, Esteban, and I had been at the park all day—sprawled out on the grass and staring up at the tall blue sky and listening to Esteban's stories of Bolivia and Russia—we all went for burgers and then drove Esteban home. When we pulled up in front of his building, we saw that the door to his apartment stood wide open.

Esteban gave a little cry and leaped out of the car, then stealthily walked to the door. He stood there listening for a while, his small body stiff and trembling. Finally, he flipped on the light and walked inside.

Jorge, Diedre, and I followed, halting just inside, shocked by the disaster that lay before us.

Esteban's narrow shoulders rose and fell with great exaggeration as he sighed.

"Que horrible," Jorge said quietly.

"Yes," agreed Diedre. "Horrible."

Esteban said nothing. Instead, he walked into the bathroom and closed the door. We could hear water running for a moment, then the toilet flush, then water running again. Finally the door opened and Esteban walked out. His eyes and his nose were red. We knew he had been crying and maybe had vomited too, but we pretended the redness did not exist, that we saw nothing but his yellow skin looking yellower beside the water-stained shade of his lamp.

Esteban began slowly picking things up off the floor and putting them back in their proper places. If things were broken, he threw them away. Without a word, we stepped inside and started helping. After we had finished, Esteban shrugged his shoulders and heaved a very long sigh.

"The CIA," he said, shaking his head in resignation. "They are very—como se dice?—persistent. Yes?"

We somberly nodded.

"Ah, well," said Esteban, reaching into his breast pocket and pulling out a small wad of tissue paper. "At least they did not take my pin. They would use it as proof, you see, of conspiracy."

We somberly nodded.

Esteban's first mugging was quick and efficient and relatively benign. He claimed it was the side effect of a jealous husband. The second mugging was slightly worse. He claimed it was the side effect of a runaway school bus which he had single-handedly brought under control and saved the lives of forty-five school children. The third mugging, however, was so bad that Esteban wound up in the hospital for three long days.

When Jorge and I first visited him there, we stepped into the cold white room and saw Esteban's bruised face and gasped, and then pretended it was the smell of medicine that disturbed us so. Esteban's wide nose had been broken and now was thickly bandaged. His eyes were swelled shut. One side of his mouth was held together with tiny black stitches. The skin over his jaws and above his brow was purple and blue and crimson. We could not see beneath the sheet, but we had heard that two ribs had been cracked, and we imagined his body to be as grimly colorful as his face.

Jorge and I stood silently next to his bed for a very long time while Esteban breathed and groaned. Finally, Jorge cleared his throat. "The CIA, my friend?"

"No," Esteban whispered through the good side of his mouth. He lifted a hand, signaling us to move closer. "Mafioso."

"Ah," said Jorge, and he nodded.

———

Esteban knew (long before Jorge or Diedre or I knew) that
love or even the possibility of love makes bad and ugly things
not so bad, not so ugly. Once, very late at night after dinner and
drinks and many yawns, Jorge leaned over and kissed me for no
specific reason. Esteban squinted a little, as if in pain, then
fished around in his pocket for a final cigarette. I leaned my
head on Jorge's shoulder and placidly yawned.

"Some day," said Esteban, in that particular tone of voice
which he reserved for philosophy and speculation, "perhaps you
will be very rich, Tamara. Perhaps you, Jorge, will be quite
famous. Perhaps both of you will have many expensive things
and will travel around the world, drinking champagne from
golden cups and watching foreign sunsets in silk robes. Perhaps
you will own more objects than you can now even imagine
owning. But even so, when you look back on this time, you will
always remember it as one of indescribable beauty. Because of
your love."

I considered this for a moment, then closed my eyes and
smiled, certain that his prediction would one day prove to be true.

And although I am sure Jorge heard Esteban's words too, he
only looked at his watch and said, *"Mirá, my friend! How very
late it is!"*

Who could know? Maybe Esteban had loved a girl in the
Soviet Union. Not a diplomat's daughter or pious Catholic mar-
tyr or ballerina spy (another story). No, a simple girl who had
the remarkable vision to see—beneath Esteban's snake-mouth
and weasel-eyes and yellow skin—an intelligent young gentle-
man of near heroic proportions. And maybe she had loved him,
too. Maybe at night as they lay together in a bed too small for
even their stunted bodies, Esteban had entertained her with
stories of adventure and intrigue and romance, and she had dis-
believed each one in turn and thus had loved him especially for
his fiction: his incredible ability to make the high walls of her
world so remote that she sometimes felt her life was without a
single boundary.

Who could know? Not Jorge, Diedre, or I. All we knew was
that no matter how fast or deliberately Esteban moved into his
future, his head seemed to be always turned over his shoulder,
staring longingly backward into a separate, secret, remarkably
happy past.

"Have you ever been in love?" Esteban asked Diedre one night
when it was very late.

We had drunk three bottles of wine between the four of us
and were sitting on the back steps of Diedre's house, staring up
at a full moon and marveling at its remarkable nearness, as if we
would not need more than a single leap to reach up and take
hold of it. It was the sort of moon that causes a vague nostalgia to rise, vague and premature, making you long for details of
simpler, happier times which you cannot yet recognize because
you're still living them.

Diedre's face was already flushed from the wine, so it was
hard to know if she blushed when she answered, "Yes, Esteban.
I have been in love. Once, years ago."

We turned to look at her, waiting for her to elaborate on an
old romance that even now seemed to lift her overweight body
up with a silent sigh. But she said nothing more.

Esteban shifted his wineglass from one hand to the other
and reached out in the pale darkness to lay a yellow hand on
Diedre's arm. "Love will come again," he told her gently. "The
world is not empty of men who see deeply, who are not blind
to beauty such as yours."

"Oh, Esteban," Diedre laughed tragically, "what a big liar
you are!"

Jorge and I gasped and held our breaths as we quickly turned
to watch Esteban's reaction. Diedre, too, was shocked by her slip
of the tongue and immediately raised two pudgy fingers to her
mouth and tapped twice as if attempting to hammer her careless
remark back inside. For although the word *liar* often surfaced in
our minds during one of Esteban's more fantastic tales, none of

us had ever said it aloud. We feared the word *liar,* feared its power to make things vanish. Or worse, break the magical spell of Esteban's imagination. Or worse yet, break Esteban himself.

Yet, perhaps Esteban had known Diedre long enough to also know that she was responding to a rare compliment the only way she knew how: awkwardly. Or perhaps he was too drunk to take offense. Whichever the case, he did not vanish, pale, or wince. Instead, he patted Diedre's arm and lifted his wineglass toward the full moon as if beginning a grand toast.

"Once, a very important man came to Russia," he said, "and I had the great fortune to share a meal with him. He was a man considered by many to be an expert on all matters of love. So, of course, I took advantage of his wisdom and asked him to give me some excellent advice on the subject. Being the agreeable man that he was, he smiled quite sweetly and told me, *Esteban, my son, the heart is a relatively durable thing. A strong heart can alter its rhythm enough to allow a man to fly to the moon and plant a flag on the moon's face. It can pump enough blood through a man's legs to allow him to reach the top of a mountain, and plant a flag there, too. It can withstand the physical strain of childbirth enough to allow a mother to plant a kiss on the cheek of her new baby.* He told to me, *Yes, my young friend, regarding matters of the body, the heart can endure much. However . . .*"

Esteban lowered his glass to take a long sip, then raised it again, turning his head to the side and squinting one eye at the moon which he had positioned in such a way that it seemed to be floating on the ruby surface of his wine. He sighed placidly and continued: "*However! Regarding matters of the soul, such as love, for example—and especially love—the heart is fragile. Very, very fragile. This is why, when speaking of love one must always speak the absolute truth.* And then this great man leaned across the table so that his nose was not more than one centimeter from mine, and he said to me, *Listen, my young friend! Listen! Although fiction can entertain the mind completely, never forget that it can also shatter the strongest heart. Completely.*"

He paused to light a cigarette and exhale a smoke ring toward the sky. We all watched the ring wobble and expand and finally vanish into the warm night air. A luna moth flitted across the moon's face. Esteban pointed at it, saying, "Believe me when I tell you, Diedre. Love will come to you again."

Diedre stared pensively at her chubby red hands and smiled. "I do believe you, Esteban."

"Ah, good," he replied, nodding his head firmly and finishing his wine in a single loud gulp.

I turned to look at Jorge who was frowning a bit, the way he always did when his mind was taking back roads and detours in order to achieve the correct answer to a very difficult question. "By the way," he asked Esteban, obviously lacking a sufficient answer, "who was this important man? This expert on love?"

Esteban paused to study the tip of his cigarette and, with the index finger of his left hand, flick invisible ashes from it.

Jorge leaned forward in his chair a bit, his eyebrows rising in unconscious anticipation.

After another flick and pause, Esteban replied: "The Pope, of course."

In September, the autumn rains began and the leaves turned brittle and fell like hoards of angels with broken wings. Jorge and I were busy with the new school year, and Diedre, who had received a promotion, was busy with her job. That is why an entire week passed before we realized that we had not received a single visit or phone call from Esteban.

It was early on a Saturday afternoon. Jorge and I had just made love and we were watching the rain and the leaves fall sadly past our window. When we grew tired of rain and leaves, Jorge got up to switch on the television. He stood there with his hands on his lovely naked hips, laughed loudly and shouted, "Come here, Tamara, and see! It is a decadent American movie!" So I got up to look at the 1970s movie with go-go girls dancing on suspended platforms, and I laughed, too.

For quite a while Jorge and I continued laughing, until we slowly became aware of a profound absence, the way one notices a chill when someone deeply loved suddenly leaves the room. Bewildered, we turned our heads this way and that, glancing into corners and through doorways. Then we understood: *Where is Esteban?*

Just then, the telephone rang and we jumped to answer it, but it was only Diedre asking, "Where is Esteban?"

We all reached deep into our memories, trying to remember if we had said anything that might have offended him, but we could recall nothing. In fact, the last time we had seen him was after a big dinner at Diedre's house and many false stories of Russia and Bolivia, and even a truly marvelous tale that took place on the streets of Calcutta, an altogether new location. Jorge and I had dropped Esteban at his apartment, but before he had unlocked his front door, he had turned to us and called out, "Jorge! Tamara! You are like family to me. Perhaps more. You know this?"

And we had called back to him, "Oh, yes, Esteban! We know! You are the same for us!"

And he had waved, and we had waved back, and as we were driving away Jorge began smiling a sleepy contented smile, so I asked him, "What are you smiling at, Jorge?"

And he answered, "Calcutta. I am looking forward to more Calcutta."

"Oh, yes," I agreed, "so am I."

But there would be no more stories of Calcutta, no more Russia, no Bolivia. The next morning as Esteban was walking to the university, three young men—big and strong and not nice at all—crossed the street to attack the vulnerable and afraid Esteban. It was his worst mugging yet.

We heard of the event from one of Esteban's neighbors, who also told us that Esteban's father had traveled all the way from Bolivia to take his son back home with him, once and for all.

We were indignant at this news and quite ready to debate the issue until we arrived at the hospital and were confronted by the impressive image of Esteban's father as he stepped from his son's room into the hallway.

Esteban's father, whom we would only know as Señor D'Angelico, was not just a handsome man. No, he was beautiful. Even Jorge, who possessed a rare South American beauty of his own, was startled by Señor D'Angelico's black almond eyes and thin straight nose and full carved lips like those on statues of perfect Roman soldiers. His hair—black, too, with blue reflections—was slicked back from his high aristocratic forehead. What's more, he stood well over six feet tall. And though he wore an expensive white starched shirt and loose-fitting gray trousers, we could still recognize the tightness of his smooth brown skin over the tightness of his muscles—even at the neck as he bent it to look at us, even at the wrist as he extended his hand to greet us. He could not have been more than forty-five years old. Not in a million years would we have guessed him to be Esteban's father.

"You are friends of Esteban?" he asked fluently, narrowing his eyes and sliding them from our heads down to our toes and up again as if we were livestock.

"Yes," we said in unison, feeling smaller and younger than we were.

"My son will survive," he said, and the ice in his voice seeped through the pores of our skin. Diedre wrapped her arms around her chest and shuddered.

"He has a fractured skull, mild contusions and lacerations and—again!—two cracked ribs. They mended him before my arrival. Unfortunate. I could have healed him without scars."

"You're a doctor," I said, not hiding the disappointment in my voice.

"A surgeon," replied Señor D'Angelico, and as if to prove this, he held out his long thin manicured hands to display their steadiness.

"Oh," I said.

Señor D'Angelico continued to admire his hands. "I do not fully understand why my son wishes to live like a raton. I send him much money, you know. Where does he put it? Not in his apartamento. No. His clothes, also, are an embarrassment. Like a beggar. A beggar! I believe that in Russia my son learned to hate money, to feel a kind of stupid shame for it. He is so easily influenced, you see . . ."

Señor D'Angelico's voice trailed off, then he snorted, "Russia! Russia. Something happened there. To Esteban. I do not know. Perhaps there was a girl . . . ?"

He dropped his hands to his sides and looked at us with an expression that shifted between disgust and disappointment. "Five times this . . . this . . . molestación has happened since Esteban came to the United States."

"We only knew about three," Diedre said sheepishly, as if ignorance of Esteban's past disproved the legitimacy of our friendship with him.

"Five," repeated Señor D'Angelico. He paused, shaking his head slowly from side to side. Not a single hair lost its place. "Five. But never again, I will make certain of this." He looked directly at Jorge. "Como un raton, sì? Like a rat?"

But Jorge did not respond to the question. Instead he asked quite abruptly, with unexpected vehemence, "Señor, do you, or do you not own a plantation?"

Señor D'Angelico tilted his beautiful head to the side and said, "No." Then he laughed, and if his voice had been full of love or kindness, it would have been a lovely sound. As it was, his laughter made us all frown when he said, "Yes, I understand. My son has been telling stories again, eh? Fantastic adventures in Bolivia? In Russia? In Africa and China and—what?—perhaps the Arctic Circle, also?"

We would have shaken our heads at the mention of the last three locations, but we did not think he really wanted an answer.

"Please forgive my son," said Señor D'Angelico, quickly sobering. "Since a small child, he is a liar. Now if you will excuse me, I must find something to eat."

And he left us standing there, looking after him as he gracefully strolled down the hallway, around a corner and out of sight.

When we entered Esteban's room, our faces must have still worn the shock of our encounter with Señor D'Angelico, because the first words out of Esteban's swollen mouth were, "You met my father?"

We nodded.

"He is quite good-looking, yes?"

We nodded.

"Like a movie star, yes?"

We nodded.

He paused for a moment, then said, as if anticipating the question we did not have the courage to ask: "I look exactly like my mother."

He raised a yellow hand to touch the gauze that wound around his skull like a careful turban, then touched a swollen cheek, the stitches on his chin. Beneath the hospital blanket, he looked so small—smaller than we had remembered him—as if his muggers had not only taken his money but a very big part of his soul.

He studied the scraped knuckles of his hand as he whispered, "My father, he told you certain . . . *things?*"

He paused.

We did not move.

"That I am a liar?"

We looked away.

There was silence.

Esteban's face contorted in a terrible grimace of pain, but we knew it was not so much physical as spiritual. Diedre moved closer and took his hand in hers, which immediately prompted tears to begin flowing soundlessly from his red and puffy eyes. The buzzing of the fluorescent hospital lights seemed terribly loud, and Jorge glowered up at them as if to frighten them into silence, but they continued buzzing. Moments passed. Jorge, Diedre, and I looked at each other as if we could somehow find a clue to what we should say next.

Finally, Jorge sighed loudly, shook his head back and forth as if disgusted, and said, "Well, my friend. It seems to me that the CIA has gone too far this time."

And Esteban looked at him sickly, then at Diedre and I, one by one, and quietly said, "Sure."

We had no way of knowing what became of Esteban after his release from the hospital. He was no longer allowed visitors after the day of our visit, and no phone calls were put through to his room. Jorge charmed a young nurse into revealing Esteban's improved condition and, finally, the date of his release. He also charmed Esteban's grouchy old landlady into allowing us to enter Esteban's apartment. The broken-down furniture remained where it had always been, but Esteban's clothes were gone from the closet, as were his few personal items—a razor, a tortoise shell comb, an old transistor radio.

Jorge, Diedre, and I stood in the middle of the chilly room and looked around with desolate faces, half expecting or perhaps wishing Esteban would suddenly appear from nowhere. Diedre's lips quivered. Jorge stuck a finger into the corner of one eye to stop a tear from escaping. I reached for the pulse at my neck, believing that my heart would, at any moment, shatter from sorrow.

Finally, Jorge cleared his throat and said, "Let's go. Esteban is gone."

As we were walking out the door, Diedre stopped, bent down and cried out, "Oh, *dear!*" Her voice choked in a sob as she held up the small, neatly folded—but empty—wad of tissue paper.

Perhaps the hollowness caused by Esteban's departure reminded Jorge and Diedre of other hollows, and so they went away to have them filled.

Diedre sold her house and moved to Los Angeles where she became, in fact, an accountant for movie stars. Hollywood changed her. Instead of furniture and fancy chocolates, she spent her money on liposuction, a nose job, and an acid treatment that burned away her purple scars forever. After she had been fully remodeled, she sent me a photograph of her new self and her boyfriend, both of whom I would have considered strangers if their names had not been written on the back.

Over the next few months, Jorge became silent and morose, so one day I asked him to leave. Which he did, kissing me good-bye on the cheek and sighing heavily from sorrow and also, I am sure, from relief. He traveled throughout Europe, then moved to Poland for a while, then to Morocco, then to a tiny village in Nepal. Wherever he went, he was able to find a woman to take care of him for the duration of his stay. (He steered clear of Spanish-speaking countries, where he was fluent and could not feign the charming accent of desperation.) After Calcutta, his postcards stopped.

I stayed where I was and married again and again, hoping to regain a thing I had lost. An elusive thing that even now seems to move further into the distance with the passing years, hand-in-hand with memories that, although still quite clear, have taken on the poignant discoloration of age.

In my favored dreams it is always spring, and the park is always new with grass, and I am always young and happy as I sit with my arms wrapped around Diedre and Jorge, all of us smiling very big smiles while we listen to Esteban weave one of his miraculous tales of adventure. And when I lean forward and whisper, "You were right, Esteban. These *were* the best days, a time of indescribable beauty," he simply waves his yellow hand through the air and says, "Do not interrupt, Tamara. I am telling you stories here. I am telling you lies."

Fog

EVEN THE BRITISH find it remarkable. In late summer when the fog is particularly dense, they drive out to this godforsaken wasteland of box houses and dwarfed palms and scrubby lawns to stand on the high cliffs above the ocean and gape at the grim miracle of it.

"Bloody amazing!" they gasp.

"Who'd've believed it?"

They shake their tweed caps from side to side, "Not I, love. Oh, do take a quick shot of me here in the gloomy heart of it."

And the cameras come out, and the poses are struck: brave hands on hips. Or trembling less brave fingers clutched tightly around woolen collars . . . nervous laughter.

Click!

Of course, the photos will never do it justice. They will be milky, underexposed, blurred from the mist-speckled lens. The tourists, however, will consider these inadequacies proof, verifiable evidence of the fog's impenetrability.

"You can very well see how extraordinarily mean it was. It did not come in on little cat's feet."

"No, wasn't the sort Mr Carl Sandburg memorialized. No, no. Wasn't that sort at all."

And the tourists will be right. No little cat's feet on this fog. This fog has hooves. It is a four-hooved beast that comes rolling

in on its backside, twisting and turning and thrashing at the sun
in a greedy vengeful fashion. Its breath is damp and cold, precisely at the lightless edge of dying.

This is how she views it:

She stands at the edge of these cliffs—the world's final
precipice—and lets the fog roll over her. What choice does she
have but to let it roll? If the tourists smile in the midst of it,
it's because they can turn and walk away, neatly tucking its wet
scent into benign memory, capturing (just as the primitives suspected) its soul in a small square of glossy paper, rendering it
powerless against them.

She stands at the cliffs' edge, too, watching from the periphery—the unobserved observer—and she envies them.

It wasn't always this way. Once the fog was new and delight-
ful. Its unavoidable presence, its visible weight, confirmed that
she had arrived in another landscape—not foreign but strange
enough, distant enough from home and dull familiarity. What
possibilities it implied! What inspiration it offered! Suddenly
there were a hundred new metaphors to steal. Suddenly there
was the tender humility of being mortal. Suddenly, the obvious-
ness of God.

Who cared about the poverty of the place, the shabby houses
with obscene colors and peeling paint, the barren lawns, the
pale gloomy children staring through drizzled windows into
blind air: that great chronic cataract of sky? In the mornings the
damp chilled walks made her skin glow pink; in the evenings
the comforting silence—or rather that ethereal whisper that
reprimanded noise and swept the streets clean of any real life.
The fog perpetuated the solitude she required. Grateful, she lent
it secret names: Mother, Lover, Breath of Saints.

Time passed.

Now she resents it: the solitude, the fog. On morning walks
along these cliffs, her shoulders stooped from the oppressive
weight of it. Her lungs suck, sputtering, at the damp air. Her
bones ache from the unforgiving cold. Her vision grows weak

from straining for a glimpse of the sun cloaked in the wet fur of this fat wild beast.

Now she sees the black mold that creeps up the walls of every room and returns—no matter how hard she scrubs—week after week. Now she sees the single palm in her front yard, a sickening pale yellow, forever stunted: What's there to stretch toward but the diminishing light? Now she sees the children who are never there with their street games of stickball and skateboards and hide-and-seek: Who could possibly find them in this overwhelming obscurity? Now she tastes the omnivorous salt gnawing at every surface: metal, weed, stone, flesh. Now she tastes the blood of her fingers. Now she hears her neighbor's sighs carried just beneath the fog's melancholy breath.

Now she hears her own voice—angry with its spent metaphors—shouting through pursed blue lips: "Look! Look at this fog like the devil's malevolent mare. Like the sepulchral shroud. Like the penitent dreams of fallen angels. Like the absence of memory. Like smoke."

Indeed: It's as if the ocean, from which we're borne, were slowly burning.

An Obscure Geography

HER CLASSROOM WAS IN THE BASEMENT of the old red-brick school where the windows looked out at the grass and skinny ankles of adolescents skipping or racing by. The windows brought in light, but we could not see the sky unless we pressed our faces against the glass and craned our necks painfully upward. Thus, standing in the square room with walls the color of pea soup, the ground seemed like a firm green liquid in which we floated, eyes bobbing just above the surface. When we took our seats, it was as if we'd drowned.

There were two spots of brightness in that dreary room. One was a perpetually changing bouquet that Mrs Patterson hand-picked from her garden or bought at the only florist in the county and then arranged in the clean crystal vase which stood on a corner of her desk. There were chrysanthemums and hyacinths and poinsettias, daisies and lilies and irises. Sometimes she'd buy half a dozen roses and have us march past them in single file to smell their sweet, heavy fragrance. We liked the bouquets. They brought us color.

So did her maps.

All eight of them were rolled up like projection screens just above the chalkboard. First was the map of the world, split cleanly between North America and Asia and drawn flat as if Galileo had never existed, as if one could indeed sail off the

edge of the earth and vanish into the blazing white nothing-
ness surrounding it. Next was the United States—first, of
course, after the world so that we children of impressionable
minds should never forget our own importance and to whom
we should ally our political beliefs. Next came North America,
then South America, Europe, Asia, Africa. Then the Pacific,
Australia, and New Zealand drawn into one.

The maps were huge. They covered the entire center section
of the chalkboard which ran the full width of the room. Even
if you sat in the back row (which was forbidden), you could
easily distinguish between Morocco and Egypt, Bolivia and
Peru. The names were printed in bold black letters, and each
country was washed in its own private color. It is the colors,
more than the names, we remembered most. Spain, for example, existed as a pleasant yellow ochre, as if it were full of nothing but sand and sunlight spreading precisely to its boundaries
and then stopping, abruptly, at Portugal's deep red surface like
a long sea of blood.

Mrs Patterson loved her maps. She loved pointing to them
with her old yardstick, hearing the wood slap the laminated
paper, and saying, "Here, people, is China. A country with millions upon millions of inhabitants . . . and all of them communists." She loved the flapping sound the maps made as she tugged
at their silver pulls and then let go, watching them disappear into
the black cylinder above. And she loved the thrill of pulling the
next one down as we migrated to another part of the world.
Those maps did not represent to her, as they did to us, the pas-
sage of time, the long school year winding its way through the
seasons and ending (as the Pacific, Australia, and New Zealand
were rolled back up) at the near edge of summer. To her they
were the unalterable anatomy of the world, something to be sure
about: the absolute geometry of land and water which would
likely outlast all of us—and, unlike us, commit no sin.

Physically, Mrs Patterson did not resemble her maps or bouquets. Her face and hands were colorless, like bleached bones,

and bore the exaggerated topography of the continents printed in the backs of our geography books. You did not have to stand very close to see the dry canyons of her wrinkles, the jagged ridge of her nose, the hollow seas beneath her eyes, the soft low rolling hills of her neck. She was tall and skinny and wore black, only black, in winter and in spring. Her hair was white. Her voice was deep and raspy. Her skin gave off the frightful odor of dying lilacs. If she sat motionless with her eyes closed, she easily might have been mistaken for a corpse.

For this reason alone we were afraid of Mrs Patterson. We did not fear her because she was strict. ("There will be no gum-chewing and no whispering and no passing notes back and forth during class or you shall bear witness to my wrath, which can be most disturbing, indeed.") Nor did we fear her because she burdened us with tough and long homework assignments, expecting nothing short of perfection from our raw little minds. ("This is incorrect, Susan. The boot heel of Missouri is straight and flat and low like the practical heel of a cowboy boot. Yours resembles the dangerous heel of—how shall I put it?—a lady of the night?")

Although we did not like the strictness or the toughness, we understood and accepted both as examples of the unyielding dedication she felt toward her students and her occupation. Yet her presence—the mere fact that she stood before us each day and we had to look at her ghastly figure—caused us an anxiety so immense that we held our breaths for most of the class period, half expecting that the contradictory glimmer of life she exuded would be suddenly extinguished before our eyes, leaving us to manage the delicate task of caring for the newly dead, a task for which we were not equipped. We were eighth graders, after all, fourteen years old. We understood even less of death than we did of life.

The county in which we all lived and went to school was small and rural and poor, but it was an easy kind of poverty, inasmuch as poverty can be easy. It was easy because so many of us had so little money that there was no shame in dressing badly or qualifying for a free lunch at school. The shame was reserved for children of the moneyed, children whose parents owned shops or funeral homes, or the few successful farms in the county which were paid for and consequently fared better than simply breaking even each year. In the grander scheme of things, these children would not have been classified as rich: They were middle class. But they had been born with more than their necessary share and thus were considered oddballs and, if they were stupid enough to flaunt what they had, outcasts.

The smarter of these children did not wear the new clothes they received at the beginning of each school year. Not right away. They waited until the trousers were a couple of inches too short, or the dresses too tight around the bust, or the sleeves too small to button at the wrists. If their parents were obsessive and threw out the old wardrobe, the children broke in the new by rolling in dirt and grass, or climbing roughly through fences and up trees. In this way, they manufactured the stains and rips of poverty and consequently feared no retribution from those of us who lived it.

In terms of this social protocol by which we all lived, Billy Casing was not smart. On the contrary, he was profoundly stupid.

He came to our school in the early spring of our eighth-grade year. His father had been an executive for a large St Louis corporation and had grown tired of being bossed around, tired of the city. He had taken the family savings and, around Christmastime, paid cash for Anderson's Hardware Store—a gloomy dusty building just off the town square which had been on the market for two years, ever since Mr Anderson had decided to retire.

Next, Mr Casing bought the Brennan place on the east side of town. It was the biggest house in the county, with three stories and fifteen rooms and an old stone fence surrounding its sprawling overgrown lawn. It had been empty for three years because old Mrs Brennan had hung herself in the attic after Mr Brennan died of cancer, and everyone suspected it was haunted. Besides, no one else in the county could afford it. The Brennan children had moved away to the city and lost touch with the reality of small-town life and asked more than the local real estate market was willing to pay for a house like that. Mr Casing did not know any better, or perhaps he did not care. He bought the house, then asked the happy real estate agent to take a picture of him standing alongside the old FOR SALE sign which now had a big new SOLD slapped across it. The agent sent a copy of the photograph to the publisher of the county newspaper who subsequently printed it on the front page because it was the biggest news that week. When everyone opened up their papers, the first thing they saw was Mr Casing looking back at them with his big-city grin, one hand on his hip, one foot resting on the post of the FOR SALE/SOLD sign like a big game hunter who'd just bagged a rare and difficult beast. The caption read: "Mr John Casing, formerly of St Louis and new owner of Anderson's Hardware Store, shows off his most recent local purchase."

People shook their heads or laughed. Some of them frowned.

After that, the first thing Mr Casing did was gut the hardware store. He put in bright fluorescent lights and new shelves and shiny metal bins for nuts and bolts and nails. He painted the walls a clean white and stripped the hardwood floor and sanded it down and added varnish until it glistened like the wet coat of a prized mare. Then he hung a sign above the front door—an enormous ugly blue and yellow thing almost as long as the building itself:

JOHN W. CASING'S SUPERIOR HARDWARE

He did not get points for modesty.

The second thing he did was renovate the Brennan house. He hired three local carpenters to steam the yellowed wallpaper from the walls and strip the woodwork and floors and paint and rebuild and rewire. He hired a landscaper from St Louis to lay out a garden, dig up the bad shrubs, trim the trees, and mend the sidewalk and stone walls.

All winter long, people slowly drove by the store and house to watch all the changes taking place. By the time spring came, the store was open for business and the house looked like new, looked as if it belonged somewhere else. In a fancy city suburb, perhaps. Certainly not in our poor county.

Finally, with the business of business out of the way, Mr Casing sent for his wife and son.

Billy was the Casing's only child, a fact for which we were seriously grateful. He wasn't particularly small, but his body still carried a stubborn residue of baby fat which made him look shorter and younger than he actually was. His eyes were tiny and closely set, and his mouth was permanently curved in an upside-down bow of petulance. He had an annoying habit of cocking one eyebrow when anyone said anything that didn't agree with him or which he doubted. He was smart, in a bookish way: He'd had the advantage of good schools and parents who read a lot and took him to foreign movies when he was very young and allowed him to watch only public television shows or listen only to public radio stations. Otherwise, he was stupid. And spoiled.

The first day of school, he walked in wearing a new shirt, new corduroy trousers, new shoes, and a new black leather belt sporting a shiny brass buckle. The shirt and trousers had been meticulously pressed, with seams so sharp you could slice a finger on them. The shoes looked wet, they were so new. And that gleaming brass buckle rode below his round stomach like a magnificent beacon, picking up sunlight through the windows and bouncing it back against the floor and walls and across the hollow eyes of students with every step he took. We stared. Billy walked straight to his locker, opened it, tossed in his books and then turned around and looked up and down the hallway. He waited until some of the noise had died down and plenty of students were looking at him, plenty within earshot. Then he turned up one side of his petulant mouth and snorted, "Jesus! What an ugly bunch of inbreeds!"

Mrs Patterson's geography class was the first class of the day. Ten minutes before the bell rang, she would take her place just outside the door and stand there in her black dress, gripping her weathered yardstick with both hands, nodding and smiling as we passed by her into the room. If we were wrestling with a friend in the hallway or leaning against a wall staring pie-eyed at a sweetheart, she would lift her head up and look down through her drooping eyelids and call out, "No dilly-dallying in the hallway, people! It's time to get down to work!" And we'd shrug our shoulders and grin sheepishly and do as she said because we knew her job was to give us reasonable orders and our job was to obey them, reasonably. Things were cut and dried like that and thus made simpler. Simpler for Mrs Patterson, simpler for us. We liked it that way.

Billy Casing, however, did not. A fact which he proved his first day of school when he showed up just as the bell began ringing, saw Mrs Patterson standing there with her old yardstick, and came to a leisurely halt right in front of her. Casually, he pressed his books to his chest and grinned a snotty grin, waiting for the bell to stop ringing. It stopped. Mrs Patterson lifted her head higher still and then turned it slightly to one side and said, "You must be a new student."

"Oh really?" said Billy. "How'd you figure it out?"

Mrs Patterson paused, and we watched her knuckles grow whiter. She spoke slowly, carefully enunciating each word—which is how she always spoke, but this time it was even slower and more precise: "I know, young man, because only a new student would be so foolish as to toy with my good nature. Risky business," she said, slapping the yardstick against her left palm. "Very risky business, indeed."

Billy snorted and said, "O-o-o-o! I'm shaking in my boots!" Then he brushed past her into the classroom and took a seat in the back row.

We all stared at him, then at Mrs Patterson, then again at Billy, waiting for what would happen next. It had been a long time since anyone had been sent to the principal's office, and even then it was for a minor offense, like sticking gum beneath a desk or passing one too many love notes. No one we could remember had ever shown a teacher such blatant disrespect. So we waited, frightened and excited, anticipating the magnificent disaster that was to come. But it didn't. Mrs Patterson walked into the room and took her seat at her desk, opened her book and looked down at it. What little color was left in her face had vanished altogether. She didn't speak or move. The big clock above the maps slipped forward five minutes.

We held our breaths. We were afraid. We thought she had died.

Mrs Patterson talked to God. She was on intimate terms with Him. She did not go to church, nor did she pray, so to speak. Rather, she held one-to-one conversations with Him: She talked, He responded. His voice, she told us, was "quite pleasant. Friendly and quick and intelligent. Like Dick Cavett." That made us feel better because those of us whose parents could afford televisions watched *The Dick Cavett Show* with regularity, and we liked him. Our parents liked him. Dick Cavett was not someone you feared.

Mrs Patterson said God first talked to her the day her husband died, eight years before, when we were only six:

Mr Patterson had been drinking, of course. He drank with notorious regularity and in notorious quantities, and when he drank he was mean. He never took a swing at anyone, but he hit people with some big-fisted insults. Every business he'd tried to start, every wild money scheme he'd invented had failed, and he blamed everyone else for causing his bad luck. He blamed Mrs Patterson for making his bad luck obvious. Drunk, he'd tell her that if she weren't so damned respected as a teacher, if she weren't the family breadwinner, then no one would care if he was lucky or not. Hell, they might even feel sorry for him and help him out a bit. As it were, they just felt sorry for her and did nothing.

He'd said this a hundred times, and a hundred times Mrs Patterson had ignored it. But on that fateful night, the night Mr Patterson's destiny scribbled THE END in his Book of Life, Mrs Patterson was tired and feeling grouchy. She spoke: "Look, here, Harvey. If I didn't win the bread then we'd both starve, wouldn't we? So why don't you just hush up about it once and for all."

Mr Patterson's face turned bright red and he broke a few more blood vessels on his nose as he shouted, "Don't you sass me, Margaret! I won't stand for no sass from no woman!"

And Mrs Patterson threw back her head and laughed, "Ha ha!" and said, "The proper grammar, Harvey, is *any* sass from *any* woman."

Well, that was it for Mr Patterson. Something ugly inside of him exploded, and he took a swing at her. Because he had never been a fistfighter, it was a bad swing. It whooshed through the air in a wide circle and kept right on whooshing, spinning him around until he lost his balance and dropped to the floor with a thud. Mrs Patterson rushed over to him and bent down and took his head in her hands and cried, "Harvey! Harvey! Speak to me! Oh, Harvey! Can you hear me?"

Mr Patterson lay there very still for a moment, then opened one eye, looked up, and spit in Mrs Patterson's face.

And that was it for Mrs Patterson. She let out a scream as if a boxer's knuckles had struck her. She jumped to her feet, raised her arms toward heaven and shouted, "Dear God, take from me this awful man! This vile, mean, horrible man! Remove him from my sight and my life! Turn him into the four-legged rat he really is!"

And God answered, "If that's the way you want it, Margaret . . . well, then, so it shall be."

Just then, Mr Patterson grabbed his head with both hands, yelled, "Ouch!" and died.

Everybody in the county knew about the rat that lived in the walls of Mrs Patterson's house. We knew she set a plate for it at her dinner table every night, that she bought cheddar cheese and saltines for it at the grocery store, that she kept a box of strychnine in her pantry—just in case. We didn't mind. In our poor little county, stranger things had happened. And because we couldn't afford most of the fancy things we saw on television or read about in magazines, we held onto our eccentricities because they were free.

Besides, there wasn't anyone who knew the world like Mrs Patterson knew it. She could tell you the altitude of any mountain, the length of any river, the width of any continent. And even though she had never traveled more than a hundred miles in any direction, she could describe the texture and color of a South American jungle in such vivid detail that when you closed your eyes you could almost hear the wild parrots, almost feel the hot, moist air. That was her special gift. She shared it with us. Out of gratitude, we did not doubt the rat in her walls. No, we believed it.

Billy Casing was an empiricist. Even before he told us what that meant, we knew it was true. When we said it was going to rain hard in March because Tommy Purkeypyle had seen a blue jay and cardinal fighting, Billy laughed, "Ha!" When we said Missy McGregor's mom was going to have a baby boy because she'd seen a raccoon washing ordinary stones in the creek, Billy cocked one eyebrow and sneered. When we said old man Scroggins had ordered himself a fine white casket because he'd heard a rooster crowing at the foot of his bed, Billy said, "What a bunch of baloney!" Then, when it rained hard in March, and Missy McGregor's mom had a boy, and old man Scroggins died the day after his casket arrived, Billy said, "Look here, you

country-bumpkin ree-tards. It rains in March, and having a boy
is a fifty-fifty chance, and Scroggins was ninety-three years old,
for Pete's sake!"

So when he told us what it meant to be an empiricist, we
looked at each other and nodded and prayed that it wasn't con-
tagious. And we also prayed that Billy would never find out
about the rat in Mrs Patterson's walls because we knew (without knowing *how* we knew) it would mean big trouble.

Mrs Patterson talked to God a lot after Billy Casing came, only
we couldn't hear the words. With the jagged end of her yardstick pointed at Thailand, she'd tell us about the tropical mon-
soons, the Buddhist temples, the simple meals of rice and fish.
Suddenly she'd stop and stare up into a dark pea green corner
of the room and tilt her head sideways as if listening. We'd wait,
breathless. Sometimes her lips would move, just barely, and we'd
strain forward over our wooden desks, trying to read them.

Being the empiricist he was, Billy Casing did not strain. He'd
sit in his forbidden back-row chair, cross his plump arms over
his chest and slide his butt forward, sinking halfway beneath his
desk. He'd squint his narrow little eyes and curl up a corner of
his pouty mouth and snort, "Crazy old witch." Generally, we ignored him, as if he were some vile but innocuous odor we were
forced to live with each day. But every once in a while some
brave kid would turn around and scowl at Billy, and he'd scowl
back in an exaggerated imitation that made him look like a
miniature demon. Which, in effect, he was.

From day one, Billy caused trouble wherever he went—trouble for teachers, trouble for students, trouble for any cat or dog
that had the misfortune of crossing his path. He created a small
explosion in science class by mixing a vial of this with a vial of
that. For English class he wrote an essay which claimed that
belief in God was a sign of mental inferiority. He "accidentally"
spilled his lunch tray on the head of little Nicky Foster, the
smallest boy in school. He tied a black ribbon around a bottle

of Lysol and hung it on Peggy Casterbean's locker. (Peggy: likely *the* poorest girl in school, who sometimes did not smell very good but was awfully nice, nevertheless.) He shot Mrs Stubble's old beagle with a BB gun while it was taking a pee on a stone corner post of the Casing's yard. And except for this last incident, for which Billy received only a gentle reprimand, Mr Casing defended his demon child and even accused the principal of picking on Billy because he was a new student. After Mr Casing inevitably threatened to file a complaint with the State Department of Education, the principal, in turn, threatened to suspend any teacher who sent Billy to his office. Thus it came to be that Billy acquired full reign of the school and Mrs Patterson acquired a virtually ceaseless dialogue with God.

Of course, we didn't yet know Billy was why Mrs Patterson and God conversed so often. We thought it was because of us, that through our piety and unswerving belief, we had made the pea green classroom into a holy place in which God could feel at home, chatting away with Mrs Patterson from His dark special corner of the room. Since we could not hear their conversations or read lips, we could not have known that God had given Mrs Patterson advance warning of her nemesis (a.k.a., Billy Casing) and had directed her to accept him as her personal Judas. This is why she did not once lose her temper with Billy, nor send him to the principal's office, nor forbid him to sit in the back row of her classroom. Billy smarted off, threw spitballs, drew hideous pictures of Mrs Patterson and taped them to the front of her desk for the whole class to see. He called her names, plucked petals off flowers in her bouquets, put thumbtacks on the seat of her chair. And through all this, Mrs Patterson simply bowed her head, closed her eyes and prayed and prayed and prayed as she literally had never prayed before.

The fact that Billy practically got away with murder made us mad and made Billy mad, too. We were mad because Mrs Patterson continued to discipline us as she had always done, possibly even more so. Billy was mad because Mrs Patterson was the only teacher he couldn't rile. She ignored him. And this, to Billy, was worse than any punishment she possibly could have inflicted upon him.

Weeks passed. Billy grew somber and quiet. He sat straight in his chair, hands folded on his desk and his round face calm, almost angelic. When a teacher called on him for an answer, he gave it—period. No smart-alecky remarks. No epithets under his breath. Just the answer, and always correct. The principal and teachers talked among themselves about the miracle that had taken place, some going so far as referring to Billy as a model student. They reasoned that the stress of being uprooted from his St. Louis home and friends and plopped down among strangers in a rural environment had caused him to misbehave. They said: "Now that he has adjusted to the changes, his rebellion is over."

But we knew better. We knew that before a tornado strikes, the air is frightfully calm. And the calmer it is, the fiercer the tornado. Mrs Patterson, who knew everything about the world, knew about weather, too. When another teacher joyfully commented to her on Billy's impeccable behavior, Mrs Patterson only smiled a kind of sick smile and grew paler, whiter— so white that she looked as if she were made of plaster, not flesh. In class, she began to fidget with her yardstick, turning it over and over in her palms, staring at it, clutching it, watching it slide over Papua New Guinea, the Solomon Islands, New Caledonia . . . and every few minutes stopping to clutch it to her breast as she looked up into the dark corner of the room to address God.

The tornado that was Billy Casing hit three weeks before school let out.

It was a warm yellow spring morning. There was a light breeze that smelled of sweet grass and new leaves and something else we could not quite put our fingers on but which reminded us of summer and the cool water of ponds and long

days with nothing to do but what pleased us. We lingered outside the front door of the school, and when the bell began
ringing we pushed our way inside and ran down the steps to
the basement, expecting to be faced with Mrs Patterson's stern
and ghostly figure pointing us into the classroom with her old
yardstick and reprimanding gaze. But the doorway was empty.

We entered and immediately stopped just inside the door,
huddling in one nervous mass of pubescence. Billy Casing
was already seated in the back row, slouching nonchalantly
like his former self and smiling a demonic little smile that
made his petulant lips stick out like two slices of a red-
skinned apple. Mrs Patterson stood with her back to the class,
facing the chalkboard and what appeared to be a large black
square of shiny paper hanging over her map of the Pacific,
Australia, and New Zealand. The air in the room felt different: bad and cold and dangerous. Even so, we moved into it,
walking toward our seats with a sense of impending doom,
our stomachs flipping upside down, our lungs without air.

Finally we sat. Only then did we realize that the shiny black
square *was* the Pacific, Australia, and New Zealand. The map had
been spray painted black, and all around it on the chalkboard
was a sparse black mist indicating the careless aim of the vandal.
Silently, Mrs Patterson reached for the formerly-silver-now-
black pull and let go. The map *flap-flap-flapped* up into the cylinder above. She pulled down Africa. It was black, too. Then Asia,
Europe, South America, North America—all of them black.

For a moment, we just stared at the back of Mrs Patterson's
head, at her hair that looked perfectly white against the perfectly black backdrop of ruined maps. Then one by one we
turned to look at Billy, none of us scowling, only gawking with
a frightened disbelief. Not frightened for ourselves, or for Billy,
or even *of* Billy. But frightened by the new knowledge that
such a heinous crime could occur in a room in which God
spoke and we could be witness to it—and then what were we
supposed to do?

Had Mrs Patterson dropped dead at that moment, as we had always feared she would, we would have been no less afraid. As it were, she remained very much alive. She let the last blackened map roll up into the cylinder, turned, grabbed her yardstick, walked straight to the back of the room and stood trembling over Billy Casing. For one long deadly-silent moment, she slapped the yardstick against the palm of her left hand and stared down at him with such a wild-angry expression that we were sure Billy would soon be dead. Billy himself must have considered that possibility, too, for his face became red, then white, then sweaty just above his upside-down-bow of a mouth that twitched a little as he tried to maintain his snotty apple-lipped smile. He slowly and carefully reached for his pencil that lay in the margin of his geography book and gripped it so tightly that it snapped in half. Finding himself weaponless, he slid down in his seat until only his eyes were visible above his desk.

Mrs Patterson smiled, but it was not a nice smile. Then she spoke: "And God said: Margaret, I'm sending you a child who will relieve the heavy burden of guilt you've carried around for eight long years. He shall be your penance, and his name shall be Billy."

She stood there a moment longer, motionless, looking at Billy but, it seemed to us, not really seeing him. Silently, we pleaded with her: *Don't walk away now, Mrs Patterson. Oh please please please do something anything to make it all right again, make it easy like it was before when the rules were simple and we were all happy.*

But Mrs Patterson could not read our minds and God did not feel obliged to tell her our thoughts, for just then she turned and walked to the front of the class, laid the yardstick on her desk, took her seat and said, "Please open your textbooks to page two hundred and seven."

Our shoulders fell. We sighed.

Billy pulled himself up and for the remainder of the class period sat with chin in hand, his little eyes narrowed and staring off into some malevolent region of space.

In the end, we didn't blame Duncan Percy for selling the story of Mrs Patterson's rat to Billy Casing. Duncan's family was awfully poor. There were nine Percy children, and none of them had winter coats or boots, and very often the only meal they ate was the free one at school. Fifty dollars could go a long way in poverty like that. And even though Duncan's trousers were raggedy and faded and permanently stained, the gleaming brass-buckled belt once owned by Billy Casing made Duncan's pitiful trousers look somewhat less pitiful.

No, we didn't get mad at Duncan. But a big part of us laid our heads down and wept. And it wasn't only Mrs Patterson we were weeping for. We were weeping for ourselves, too. We had discovered that we were corruptible. Like the ugly stupid hopeless bad guys on TV or in books, we could be bought.

The last week of our eighth-grade year we stared at Duncan Percy strutting down the hallway and coveted the beacon of light that shined from his brass buckle into our hollow eyes. We coveted, too, the candy that bulged inside his tattered pockets and we followed him around, waiting for some of it to spill through the holes onto the floor. Which it did. And then we'd scurry after the sweets like a pack of hungry rats.

We were saddened by our greed, and we were afraid, too. Only this time our fear was bigger wider longer than any fear before it.

We sat in Mrs Patterson's classroom on the last day of eighth-grade, trembling, waiting for her to arrive, staring at the blackened maps of the world and longing for the clear boundaries, the boldface names, the bright colors of here and there and somewhere else, longing for the concrete, for God with his comforting Dick Cavett voice, but confronted instead by the shiny black unknown of a world that, for us, had been irrevocably changed. (Billy Casing was conspicuously absent that last day. Mr Casing felt it was best to keep him home, considering the circumstances.)

It was fifteen minutes after eight when Mrs Patterson finally walked in. Her arms were full of roses—pink ones, red ones, yellow ones, white ones. She placed them on top of her desk and as she called the roll, she asked us to please come up and take one.

"Now, be careful of the thorns, people," she said in her precise locust-buzz of a voice. "Don't prick your fingers on them. And don't use them as weapons against your neighbor. Such behavior is not permitted in my class."

After roll was taken, she folded her hands on her desk and looked out at us with a steady and stern gaze. Everyone except Missy McGregor held their breaths. Missy sat in the front row, crying and sniffling and wiping her nose on the sleeve of her old dress, knowing instinctively what was to come.

Finally, Mrs Patterson spoke. "As you all may have heard, I will be retiring after this year."

We nodded gravely.

"It is not an action I have chosen, but one which was forced upon me by the school board. Their decision, I feel, is unjustified and irrational. I am not, nor have I ever been, mentally unstable. Nor do I consider myself a danger to my students. If I suffer from any affliction then it is simply one of perpetual loneliness and grief. Certainly not of madness. Now," she said standing, "since summer vacation begins tomorrow and not today, we shall have one final lesson in geography."

Out of respect, we did not let loose our usual groans. Instead we pulled our shoulders straight and folded our hands on our desks and set our jaws firm and opened our eyes very wide, as if our body's posture of eager attentiveness would allow our souls to absorb the whole of Mrs Patterson's knowledge.

From her desk drawer she pulled a large folded square of paper and opened it up. It was a map of the world, dingy and yellowed and cracked at the folds. She taped it onto the chalkboard and then picked up her yardstick and lightly touched it against the map.

"Listen up, people," she said loudly, although we were heedful and silent. She held her sunken chin high and regal and did not tremble or shudder or quake.

"Maps," she began, "are lonely things. Desolate abstractions of the world. A world which is never so tidy as the clean boundaries the cartographer draws between one country and the next, one continent and the next—the land a bright shade of earth or stone, the water always blue. *Where are the people?* one might ask. I respond: Only God can fill in the lives that come and go, that have come and gone—tiny lights springing up across the flattened globe of the world and then sputtering, waning, flickering, going out. And so much between the springing up and dying away. And so many lights."

She turned toward us briefly, then away.

"And where, people, where are your lights? In this hemisphere, this continent, this country, this state, this county, this small pinpoint of a town which is the only world you know and is not even labeled. . . . Where are *your* lights? *Your* lives?"

She looked at us.

We looked at her. Even though we were almost freshmen, we did not have an answer for a big question like that.

Of course, Mrs Patterson who knew so much, knew our limitations, too. She let her yardstick slide from the map and smiled. "That is your homework assignment, people. Tuck it into your pockets and carry it with you always. And every now and then, when you feel you have grown too comfortable with yourselves, pull it out and see if you've found the answer yet."

Then her mouth opened and she took a breath but no words came out. Her face grew very white, whiter than we had ever seen. Her eyes blinked once, then twice, then closed. She fell to the floor.

We all leaped halfway out of our seats, then froze with our mouths open and our eyes bulging. The clock above the chalkboard ticked loudly. The fluorescent lights hummed. Through the open window, the breeze carried the sound of a hand mower rolling across the green sea of the school lawn. Finally, little Nicky Foster stood all the way up, walked around his desk to the front of the room, bent down and disappeared behind Mrs Patterson's desk. We sat down again and waited.

His little head popped up and he looked at us. "I think she's dead," he said calmly.

Peggy Casterbean, who rarely spoke, asked softly, "What should we do?"

Tommy Purkeypyle said, "I think somebody should go tell the principal."

We all nodded.

"Who wants to go?" asked Nicky.

"I will, I will!" cried Missy McGregor, raising her hand high in the air. She stood up and began to step away from her desk, then remembered her rose, picked it up and walked out of the classroom with her nose pressed against the soft white petals.

On the first day of our freshman year we skipped study hall, pooled our money and ran to the florist to buy a bouquet for Mrs Patterson's grave. The sum of our pocket change could not have purchased more than a half-dozen tiger lilies, but the florist loaded our arms with a dozen roses each. Mrs Patterson had been, after all, his best customer.

The day was hot and humid. The cemetery lawn had just been mowed and the grass smelled sweet—not like death at all, but like something new and hopeful. We spread the roses over the dry dirt of Mrs Patterson's grave, then tossed the left overs onto the grass and weeds of Mr Patterson's grave. Because we did not know much about giving eulogies, we stood there in awkward silence, watching rose petals wilt beneath the hot August sun. Finally Tommy Purkeypyle cleared his throat and said, "The capital of Alaska is Juneau."

We stared at him. Then we understood.

Nicky Foster, who'd grown three inches over the summer, said in his new deep voice, "The Amazon River is 3,915 miles long."

One by one we stepped forward and rattled off state capitals, foreign cities, mountain ranges, rivers and lakes and seas and oceans, some of us stating facts we didn't know we'd learned. And we could have kept stating, too, but just then Duncan Percy pushed his way to the graveside and stood there trembling in his raggedy clothes, his old trousers still hoisted by the brass-buckled belt, though the buckle no longer shined like new.

With tears pooling in the hollows of his eyes, he pulled back his shoulders and said, "I know geography, Mrs Patterson. I know I'm standing here, and it don't make no difference if this place ain't on no map. I can see it plain as day. It's where I am, Mrs Patterson. Where I live. And Billy Casing? Well, he lives someplace else. Always did. Always will."

We all nodded and said, "Amen," because of all the facts we knew, this one was likely the truest.

Shortly after Mrs Patterson's funeral, a scrawny lice-infested rat took up residence in the attic of the Casing's house. They hired a local exterminator to get rid of it and when that didn't work, they hired one from St. Louis, but the rat stayed on. Mrs Casing claimed she'd seen it on more than one occasion, squatting at the foot of Billy's bed while he slept. When Mrs Stubble stopped by to say, "You ain't never gonna git rid of that rat, Mr Casing, sir, 'cause it ain't no ordinary rat," Mr Casing had snorted and cocked one eyebrow and laughed, "Ha!" Nevertheless, he put the house and hardware store on the market the following week because Billy had come down with a nasty skin rash that made him scream and cry and itch and eventually bleed. And Mrs Casing, who'd become suddenly and fiercely religious, insisted it was a sign from God.

Where All Things Converge

Without sex, I believe I am as invisible and real as humidity on a hot Missouri day. I believe I pass unseen through crowds, causing moisture on the brows of young men. Celibate, I make life miserable for women: I walk by and they suck in their bellies and tilt their breasts upward. I imagine they wish they'd put on a different dress, perhaps a brighter shade of lipstick . . .

EACH SUNDAY for the past three weeks I've had lunch with the same man. Reuben is not handsome by any means, although his clothes fit nicely about his hips, which are narrow for a man his size, and square. When he wears tight jeans, they look as if they were carved from stone; they look powerful. Without a doubt, Reuben's hips are the most interesting feature about him.

We meet at the museum cafeteria. He is always early. I am always late. I don't know why I have never suggested another lunch spot. The cafeteria gives me vertigo. It was designed to resemble a Roman courtyard. The architecture is obscenely large. Thick columns rise fifty feet on all sides past an upper balcony, toward an immense skylight. There is a large fountain in the center of the floor which produces an irritating drizzle like an incessant rain. The potted trees near the tables look fragile and dwarfed against the high walls. There is too much space. When I turn my head quickly, I feel as if I'm flying.

Today I am only ten minutes late, and Reuben is already seated at our usual table. He sees me standing in the doorway and waves. I am wearing dark sunglasses, thinking they might ease my dizziness.

I look exotic in sunglasses, like a woman with a dangerous past. When I walk across the tiles, men raise their eyes and grow quiet. Their wives or girlfriends try to divert their gazes by quickly speaking or touching their rough hands. I sit down and a woman at the next table looks away. She bows her head, her chin almost touching her collarbone, and carefully smooths the silk of her blouse.

Reuben beams at me and draws his chair close. "So," he asks, "how was your week?"

"Unremarkable," I reply.

I look to see how long the line is to the buffet table. It is very long. It curls around the columns and flattens against the back wall of the courtyard. No one standing there looks relaxed, no one looks comfortable. The men put their hands in and out of their coat pockets and check their wallets distractedly. The women hold their purses in front of them with both hands, looking frightened. Everyone solemnly faces outward, toward the center of the courtyard, as if about to be executed.

"What would you like to eat today?" Reuben asks.

"What's on the menu?"

"The same. It's always the same on Sunday."

"Fine," I say, yawning. "I'll have the same as last week."

Reuben rises from his chair slowly, trying not to bump the table. His jeans are tight today and worn strategically thin in places. Still bent, his legs press against the denim and a hard muscle bulges from his thigh, continuing upward toward his pelvis. I wonder what it would be like to have hips like his, solid and compact. I imagine being able to lock into the earth like old tree roots, being able to run very fast and naked. With those hips, I believe a person could carry the world for years and never grow tired.

Reuben hesitates beside the table, watching people moving slowly through the buffet line.

"Awfully long today," he says, frowning. He is nervous. He knows how ridiculous everyone looks standing shoulder to shoulder like birds on a high wire. He knows he will probably do the same, not wanting to be different, not wanting to stare into the profile of the person ahead of him. My friend is not a rude person.

"Want me to go with you?" I ask with uncharacteristic altruism.

He wants to say yes. "No, it's not necessary," he says instead. "Maybe the line will move faster today."

I watch him tug upward on his belt loops. I want to tell him that I would be proud to stand in any line if I had hips like his. In fact, I would consider it my duty, waiting among a hundred ordinary anatomies, to show these people how an old pair of jeans can be transformed into something ethereal.

Reuben straightens his shoulders and moves toward the line. My eyes grow moist behind my sunglasses.

I once had a terrible argument with a hopelessly logical woman about love and obsession. She told me she refused to have sex with large-nosed men. She said that although her nose was small and shapely (the result of rhinoplasty, I later discovered), her family had a history of impressive snouts.

"Christ, just imagine it," she said dully. "I get pregnant by some guy with a big schnauze and all those indelicate genes come funneling down into a kid who looks like my grandfather. God forbid I should have twins."

I told the woman (who has since married a beautifully nosed man and had three beautifully nosed children) that physical appearance alone was a lousy reason to avoid sex with any man. I said that when I fell in love, it was because of what the man held within him. "An unseen beauty," I said, "like a palmed jewel."

I told her: "I have never fallen in love with a man simply because of the way he looked."

But that was a lie.

When I was twenty, I fell in love with a political science student because he looked wonderful in his overcoat. The coat was black and heavy and much too large for his lanky build. When he wore it with a scarf and hat, I thought he looked like a 1940s intellectual, like a man with significant dreams. I imagined him alone on darkening street corners, passing out hand-printed leaflets, his beard gathering ice in the cold. We discussed marriage. I thought we would make an attractive couple: the intense man who was going places and the beautiful woman following him. I thought our children would be compassionate and wise, would correct social injustice and end wars. At twenty, I was a dreamer.

Then the spring came and the man put the overcoat into storage and something was lost. It was as if all my illusions at the time were contained in the fibers of that coat, and the coat gave those illusions density and form. It defined my idealism completely.

Coatless and in a crisp oxford shirt, the man looked like a Republican. He became president of the student body and I became a cynic.

Reuben is virtually my last link with male civilization. He is safe. What he demands of me is a Sunday lunch and an easy conversation, neither of which is too difficult for me to handle. What I can't handle is romance, or rather the illusion of romance. Call it by any other name—lust, animal magnetism, the heavy unavoidable scent of pheromones—and maybe I'd consider handling that, too. But I've yet to meet a man who can call a spade a spade. If I do, then perhaps I'll change my celibate ways. Meanwhile, there's Reuben, who is safe.

He is an intelligent man, although he says I often make him feel ignorant and childish. He says I have a way of looking at him during conversation that makes him wonder if he's speaking nonsense. I tell him he's being paranoid. He tells me I am probably right. Reuben rarely disagrees with me, which is sometimes annoying. (I don't like feeling as if I've been granted a license to say anything I please. The temptation to lie becomes too great.) He says he rarely disagrees with me because I am rarely wrong. I say it's because he doesn't like making waves. For example:

Last Sunday as we were leaving the museum, Reuben dropped his wallet while trying to shove it into his back pocket. As he was bending down to pick it up, a small boy came racing around the corner and ran into him, sending them both sprawling across the hard marble floor. Reuben's glasses were knocked from his face and broke precisely in half. The boy's mother witnessed the collision and instead of scolding her son, she walked up to my friend and began swearing at him for his clumsiness. Reuben silently studied the halves of his glasses.

The woman yanked her son from the floor and stomped out of the building. The boy followed her closely, looking sheepishly over his shoulder at us. Reuben winked at him. The boy grinned.

"Jesus," I said. "What a bitch! Why in hell did you let her get away with that? Why did you just stand there and let her humiliate you?"

"Arguing wouldn't have solved anything," said Reuben. "Besides, the boy was embarrassed enough as it was."

I sighed in dismay. Reuben smiled and patted me on the head.

To my left, a good-looking bearded man is smoking a pipe and watching me through the blue smoke. He is older, perhaps fifty, and wears a dark blue suit. It is the same man who has sat at that same table, watching me, for the past three Sundays. I turn my head away and scrutinize him out of the corner of my eye. He takes the pipe from his mouth and tips it at me like a hat, then grins lecherously. I feel as if I am slowly becoming visible again and tell myself I should buy sunglasses with mirrored lenses.

Which reminds me.

In college I took a short seminar that focused on the mental disorders of older adults. Near the end of the course, the class visited a local clinic that was researching premature senility. We were allowed, three at a time, into a small examination room separated from the testing room by a two-way mirror. For fifteen minutes I stood and watched a forty-year-old man undress, grow confused, and put his clothes back on. The student standing next to me in the room said he was becoming depressed and asked to leave. But I was fascinated.

The subject was a huge man, well-endowed, who looked as if he might have been a truck driver or member of a 1960s motor-cycle gang. His chest was covered with tattoos. A long purple scar cut across the inside of his thigh. Yet there was a definite grace about him, a fluidity of movement which made his little ritual of undressing more like a surrealistic dance than a symp-tom of Alzheimer's disease.

I watched him with a sort of perverse excitement, like a peep-ing Tom watching a homely woman touch her small breasts, and smiling. The man undressed and redressed, oblivious to my presence and oblivious to any identity he may have held of him-self before his illness. I was invisible to him, he was invisible to himself, and yet I was witness to both.

There is a kind of power inherent in voyeurism, a feeling of absolute control. For the past sexless year, I have watched myself become both the man undressing and the perverse woman watching—*and* the invisible woman who understands invisibil-ity, and smiles.

While my head is turned, Reuben slips into his chair and places a tray of food on the table. I'm disappointed I missed his arrival: When he sits, his hips press forward a bit and the folds in the crotch of his jeans are drawn tight.

"Your salad," he says, arranging the plate and tableware in front of me.

"Thank you."

"Are you still on a diet?" He asks this with averted eyes. I imagine someone once told him this is the polite thing to do.

"Only during the day," I tell him. "At night I go home and binge. I sit in front of the television, reading and eating. I eat from the time I get home to the time I go to bed."

His eyes widen. "I'm amazed you stay so thin."

"Thin," I say, "is not a good word to describe me."

"You look fine," he says. "Thin is a good word."

"My ass is too big."

"Your ass is wonderful." He quickly looks at his plate.

When Reuben is embarrassed his ears turn a brilliant red. To conceal their radiance, he places a hand flatly over the ear facing me. He does this casually, leaning an elbow on the table as if resting his head.

Reuben is embarrassed because he knows that talking about my ass or breasts or eyes bores me. He knows I've heard it all before: that my ass is like a generous moon, that my breasts rise like new species waiting to be named, that my eyes are the loyal confidantes of the world. He knows, too, that there are those who take credit for another's beauty simply by having defined it. He knows, for example, that a woman who discovers the miracle of a man's hips believes she possesses them.

I change the subject: "How is your play coming along?"

"It isn't."

I notice he is not really eating. He is simply moving his peas from one side of the plate to the other, one at a time.

"You've hit a dry spell?"

"Maybe. I'm having a hard time concentrating on it. My mind wanders a lot lately."

His mind is wandering now. There is a tense, distracted look in his eyes, and I've seen that look a hundred times in a hundred men who believed they were falling in love with me, who believed that what they were feeling was something more profound than simply a surprised libido.

But Reuben is a smart man. He knows that if he mentions the word *love* I will sigh or yawn and he will have to bury his red ear in his hand. I decide to rescue him from his dilemma by excusing myself from the table.

This morning I found my diaphragm beneath the bathroom sink. I took it from its storage case and held it up in the light. The rubber was dry and brittle and beginning to discolor. When I squeezed the rim between my thumb and index finger, the center split open like a small hemisphere giving way to hidden fault lines. I sighed.

The nurses at Planned Parenthood tell you that if you have frequent intercourse or are prone to sexual acrobatics, your diaphragm can tear and thus be rendered useless. They tell you that a weight gain or loss of ten pounds is reason enough to have your diaphragm replaced. They do not tell you, however, that a diaphragm which remains unused for a long period of time will lose its suppleness, will eventually turn to dust.

I threw the diaphragm into the wastebasket and imagined my ovaries turning to dust, my vagina losing its suppleness, going dry. But it was an absurd thought: My ovaries still ache every month. My vagina is still moist and yielding.

Without sex, I think my body heals the old scars, forgives itself the tissues lost to abortion. Celibate, I imagine growing clean and tight as a virgin: I hold the world in the palm of my hand. Or hold it, rather, in another more discreet part of my anatomy.

In the bathroom of the museum, a woman in a blue dress stands at the sink washing her hands. She is small and attractive, in her late thirties. When I enter, she turns her head toward me and I smile. The side of her mouth twitches in a feeble attempt to return my gesture. When I come out of the toilet stall, she is retouching her makeup. I move to the sink to wash my hands and she quickly drops her lipstick into her purse. (I have never worn lipstick. My lips are a deep red and their edges clearly defined. They are full in the center and turn up at the corners. Even unhappy, I look as if I've just been laid.) She takes a brush from her purse and begins running it through her short brown hair. She glances at my reflection in the mirror. When I bend down to turn off the faucet, my long red hair falls around my shoulders like an exotic shawl. She brushes harder.

I move around her to dry my hands. "That's a beautiful dress," I tell her.

She tosses the brush into her purse and slings it over her shoulder. "Easy for you to say," she hisses and walks out of the bathroom.

Her heels click on the marble floor like a tap dancer's.

A friend of mine, who is neither pretty nor homely, can't hold a conversation without eventually bringing up the subject of ugliness. She is a painter. For the past three years she has painted nothing but horrifying self-portraits in various degrading positions. The features of her face are usually distorted beyond recognition, and the images of her vulva—rendered in luminous pinks and greens—resemble malignant growths or dangerous insects. I hate these paintings and tell her so every chance I get. This seems to please her a great deal.

"Ugliness," she says in a voice filled with true piety, "is a state of being. When I imagine my own ugliness, I see it as being complete, as going beyond the flesh."

"You're not ugly," I always tell her.

"I *am* ugly," she always replies. "Look, sweetie, wherever I go, people call me *sir,* and even then they're not certain they've got it right. True ugliness isn't easily defined."

I tell her: "People call you sir because your hair is cut short and you're very tall. When my hair was short, I was often mistaken for a man."

"That's a lie."

"You're right," I say. "No one has ever mistaken me for a man. But let me tell you something, it's not easy being beautiful.

Women hate you and men haunt you. A truly beautiful woman can never enjoy absolute anonymity. Take me, for example."

"Oh, god," my friend always says, "you are *so vain!*"

"Do you think I'm vain?" I ask Reuben the moment I reach the table.

Reuben, caught with a mouthful of mashed potatoes mumbles something incoherent.

As I lean over the table to sit his eyes peer down my blouse at my breasts. His pupils dilate. Like a smart detective, he quickly glances at the fiftyish bearded man with a pipe who is also peering down my blouse. The man sees Reuben watching him, takes three long puffs on the pipe and disappears behind a cloud of smoke. Reuben scowls and scoops up a huge mound of potatoes. It is an unpleasant male exchange I have witnessed too many times to receive much pleasure from anymore.

"Well?" I demanded.

"Well what?" The potatoes are poised seductively before his mouth. Reuben has a lovely mouth. I've just discovered this. Open, the lips curling outward, his mouth looks as if it could fold around any geometry. And the geometry, grateful, would let itself be swallowed whole.

"Do you," I repeat, "or do you not think I'm vain."

In one agonizingly slow movement, Reuben sucks the potatoes into his mouth. My eyes blink rapidly behind my sunglasses. My cheeks flush. He swallows and wipes a napkin across his chin.

"I don't think you're vain," he says. "I think you're honest. If you denied your beauty, you'd be a liar. Besides, vanity speaks with a smile or a sigh. When you talk about your breasts or ass or eyes, you *sneer.*"

I raise my eyebrows above my sunglasses. Reuben looks at me, grinning.

Throughout my youth I wanted to be beautiful. When I was nine, I told God I would become a nun if He would mold me

into an astonishing woman. At nine, I did not realize the poten-
tial conflict of interest in being a nun *and* beautiful. But I
knew I wanted to be adored. I wanted a pedestal high enough
that men could look up my skirt and give thanks to God's
earthly wonders.

There were two painfully long years just before puberty
when the fate of my physical appearance seemed disastrous. In
those two years, I grew five inches and gained only three
pounds. My legs resembled new saplings; my ass, an incomplete
gesture. And my breasts—*oh my breasts that ignored expensive
creams and tedious hours of bust exercises*—could have been contained in two spoons. Then, in the spring of my fourteenth year,
only months after I'd bled through my bathing suit at summer
camp, God or heredity came through for me: My flesh shifted
over the long bones like sand in Egypt. It swelled and pressed
against the world, subtracting volume from air. It defied gravity
while proving it: My breasts, huge and perfect, rose above my
ribs and pointed like two compass needles to True North, to my
magnetic future waiting for me with a damp crotch. *In all its
glory, my sexuality shone in my eyes and told the world it had arrived
and it was good.*

It was a religious experience, no doubt. But by that time I'd
become an agnostic and no longer felt obligated to my monas-
tic vows.

In those early years, I enjoyed my beauty and took advantage
of it. I didn't need a pedestal; metaphorically speaking, men fell
on their knees before me, awed by the wet grace of my thighs.
They slipped their hands up my skirt and wept in gratitude. I let
them come inside me and felt beneficent. If I would not turn
my soul over to God, I thought, then the least I could do was
offer up my body to His men, who seemed to be healed by it.
But I grew tired of my own generosity. Tired of the men so thick
at my feet and ass that I couldn't breathe. I felt like a temple full
of thieves tearing gold from the altar and then carving their ini-
tials into the walls before leaving. Even untouched I felt violated:

On a bus, a fellow passenger followed me across town. He got off with me at my stop and walked the four blocks to my house, always keeping a distance of ten feet between us. When I reached my front door I quickly turned and asked him what the hell he thought he was doing. He told me he had never seen any woman quite as stunning and simply wanted to *bask in the light of my magnificence.* I rolled my eyes toward heaven and told him to go to hell. The next day I cut off all my hair and began wearing men's clothing one size too big. But it changed nothing. The men still haunted me like regretted pasts.

Real beauty, I concluded, is difficult to disguise.

I remove my sunglasses and give Reuben a hard stare. To my surprise, he does not turn away but places a hand over mine. It is cool and sleek as a pianist's. I imagine it dancing over the white keys, over skin smooth and wet and obliging, and the skin picking up the light rhythm like a deft partner.

My fingers twitch beneath his.

He says, "It's not our fault, you know."

"What's not whose fault?"

"Men, and the way we lap you up with our eyes, wishing it were our tongues instead." His hand trembles and there is a slight burning in his cheeks. "Always thirsty, we're drawn to moisture. Sex rises from you like steam."

"I know," I sigh. I slip my hand out from under his and touch my knee to his thigh. "But it's not my fault, either. I've tried to put a lid on it, so to speak. I've cut off my hair, dressed like a bag lady. Once I even went a week without bathing and then a man grabbed me on the street one day and said, 'Lady, your fragrance could make a priest stumble over his robe.'"

Reuben nods and presses his leg harder against my knee. "God and sex," he says. "That's what we seek. The misguided seek God and believe sex will move them away from discovering Him. The smart ones, they look for sex and find it and know that as they hover over that one deliciously wet spot of the world, they're as close to God as they'll ever be."

"So which are you?" I ask.

Reuben grins. "I'm smart."

There is a humming inside me as if a train were passing close by. Reuben cautiously slips a hand beneath my skirt and slides it up the length of my thigh. The tablecloth flutters.

The bearded man walks by our table, brushing against my shoulder as he passes. He winks.

"God and sex," Reuben repeats.

I nod and fold my damp thighs around his dancing fingers and close my eyes: I imagine a train moving past me, so close I think I could reach out and run my fingers along its smooth steel. The ground shifts beneath my feet.

And as I hover over that one gloriously wet spot of the world where all things converge, I see a woman on that train. She is huge and visible as light and resembles me. She stands at the window and turns, pointing her perfect breasts to True North where I wait. I call out to her and she flies past me like a dream, smiling and waving.

Our Perversions

(QUANTUM FICTION)

The world thus appears as a complicated tissue of events, in which connections of different kinds alternate or overlap or combine and thereby determine the texture of the whole. —Werner Heisenberg
Physics and Philosophy

Dear **X**:

You say you want something greater than sex, exigent, more profound. You say: *Sex cannot fully define the human condition.* It is a trivial matter, and base—a residue of our primitive past. I agree. And yet. What greater human tragedy is there than unquenchable desire? The constant striving to fill or be filled? Even as I write this, I imagine licking the salt of your neck.

I SEE YOU, forever standing on the whitewashed balcony overlooking the sea where the sad gray dinghies bob and sway, sails torn from their masts, and staring beyond them at the tentative arc that separates water from sky.

Tentative arc: *me as water, you as sky. The sky slides into the water, the water swells, the sky becomes wet. We moan, sigh. Do we also weep?*

On the whitewashed balcony you stand smoking a cigarette. You are shirtless, barefoot, tan. Your trousers hang loose about your hips, below the small of your back that is perpetually moist and warm: a tender hollow where I press my hands when you lie upon me and gently part my legs with your knee and find my sex with your own—a determined crusader searching for the arc of perpetual life—and then poise one trembling moment before slipping inside me, searching my eyes for the unspoken word of astonishment, always astonished by your breadth, the hot unavoidable presence of you in me, and then you move, tentatively at first, then deeper as I pull you up by the small of your warm damp back, up and in—me the conductor, you the musician—synchronizing your moans, deep and quiet with each slow thrust: "Uhn . . . uhn . . . uhn . . ."

> Dear **X**:
>
> We are broken apart, you and I. In sex we rejoin, but only fleetingly. The wounds of our differences do not entirely heal; they gape and seep the moment we roll away from each other. Thus we spend our separate lives attempting to distract ourselves from the pain of who we are in solitude. Still, you will agree: Desire that must be controlled controls us. Dreams are an excuse to abandon control. I dream of you sucking my tongue while you lunge inside me. You dream of me arching like a soft green tree as I open my lips for your inguinal passion. Thus desire wins, reminding us again and again that it exists.
>
> When I awaken, I want you. And I don't even have to know your name.

You stand on the whitewashed balcony smoking a cigarette, your brown hands gripping the chalky railing, the fulcrum of your leaning into the breeze that tousles your fine black hair: the way it smells when it is damp when I kiss it when it falls across my breasts.

I look at you standing on the balcony, at the nape of your neck where fine black hairs form a v, an arrow that points to the tip of your spine that snakes down between the fleshy muscles of your shoulders that twitch from some unnecessary reflex as a seagull swoops low, descends into your periphery and hovers there, stiff winged, upon the breeze that sweeps from the sea across the shore and up the dunes to where you stand on the balcony oblivious to the gull that hovers at your periphery because your mind is not on the balcony where your body leans into the breeze, toward the sea and past it, as if pressing toward the inevitable future: *When you come I disappear into the little death you suffer each time you reach the place you are moving toward: your little death. Your painful, pleasurable, insouciant, fleeting little death.*

The cigarette in your right hand burns close to your knuckles. You raise the cigarette to your lips, drag on it long and deep, then exhale. The gull rises, borne on a simple cloud of smoke and wind, and disappears over the rooftops. You flick the cigarette over the balcony onto the sand below. You run your fingers through the fine black hair of your head. You squint and sigh.

You turn.

And for a moment you do not see me as you enter the room that still smells of sweat and sex and something else unnamable, sumptuous, but see still the vision that fastened your eyes to the horizon. Then it vanishes: the vision, the horizon. And you halt as if startled. Startled by my presence in the room, on the bed, naked, gazing at you, at your black eyes wide and startled, as are mine: startled by the feet polished by sand, the hard-soft hips, the fine black hairs curling above your trousers toward your navel, your stomach, your slick chest with its tense nipples and pillowy aereolas, your wide shoulders, your thick neck, your face with its palatable lips and aquiline nose and eyes intense and startled below the fine black hair of your head until you recognize the room, the bed, me.

"You are exquisite," you say.

You are exquisite. Your body intense and scrupulous. The shape of your soul.

With two fingers you unbutton your trousers. They fall to the floor.

"What are the chances?"

"If you believe in predestination, then the chances never alter. They are always in your favor. Things will happen as they were meant to happen. To be surprised is to doubt inevitability."

"It is inevitable we met."
"It is inevitable we speak of inevitabilities."

You did not wish to attend the exhibition. The crowds, the laughter: the loneliness they imply. But you had promised the artist, and like nightmares, your promises are honorable. You dressed carelessly: an unpressed shirt, trousers stained with a spot of paint on the thigh, a thin crust of mud on the left heel of your boot. You combed your fine black hair, but when the wind outside disheveled it, you did not bother to comb it again. You went to the exhibition.

You paid your respects to the artist, friends, acquaintances. You studied the paintings on the walls. One in particular caught your eye: a woman, nude, sprawled upon a bed beyond which two doors opened onto a balcony overlooking the sea. The sea and the sky. A tentative arc of line between them. The woman on the bed smiling faintly as if remembering the scent of a man who has just left the room. You thought you could hear seagulls calling across the waves, hear the waves, too, rolling onto the shore.

What was it you felt then? Longing? Melancholia? Nostalgia for a moment that had not yet occurred?

Your face drawn in sadness as you turned from the painting and moved toward the door where I stood gazing at a painting of a man rising out of water and the water shimmering as it falls from his slick brown skin like electrons finally captured within their nebulous paths, and the sun on the water, and the sky on the water, and the water gazing up at the sun and the sky.

I stood near the door in front of a painting of a man rising out of water that evoked the same melancholia, loneliness, nostalgia for what had not yet occurred, and I said without turning to you, knowing you were near: "See how quickly the water engulfs the absence left by the rising man, as if to battle the sadness of his leaving."

———

I whispered, "Don't go."

You smiled, "I'm not leaving."

"Stay inside me. I can't bear the hollow of your absence."

And so you lay between my legs, atop me, until we fell asleep and dreamed simultaneous dreams of unrippled seas.

Your voice rises in a question that mirrors my own. "We've met before?"

"It's possible," I say, "though I can't recall . . ."

But something shifts within my internal vision, and I briefly catch the memory of you standing in a moment that has not yet occurred, can smell the heat of your skin, taste your salt on my tongue.

Must we always remember the past? Must we always be limited to the memories of what has already occurred? If I think I know the flesh between your fingers is soft and white, can it not then prove soft and white? If I think I know the exact proportion of down upon your buttocks, when I later slide my hands across your buttocks cannot the proportion of down be exact?

As if to satisfy my queries, you say, "I think you've been waiting for me a long time."

"Years," I say.

"Then the wait is over."

Is it?

You sat on the edge of the bed, naked except for a pearl of sweat that loosened itself from your collarbone and slid down the center of your wide brown chest and nestled itself in your navel. I got down on my knees and spread your thighs apart and pressed my lips over your navel to suck the pearl from it. You smelled like the sea. And the salt of the sea mixed with the salt of you, and I could hear the waves slapping against the sand beyond the balcony doors, hear the gulls reeling over the rooftops, the sigh of the wind holding the gulls aloft like the breath of God beneath wings of angels. And you cupped my head in your hands and slowly lifted it until I could see you were weeping, your smile quivering between exultation and anguish. And so I stood and kissed the salt of your tears that fused with the salt of your sweat that fused with the salt of the sea, and you gasped and buried your face between my breasts.

Your fine black hair: the way it smells when it is damp when I kiss it when it falls across my breasts.

With my hands clutching your shoulders, I climbed onto your lap and wrapped my legs around your hips, and you slipped your hands beneath my bottom and maneuvered me close: my sex touching your sex that stood erect and poised upon the threshold of my own salted wetness, and you whispered, "Look at me." And I looked. And you whispered, "See me, see all of me, see all of who I am." And I saw. And when you saw that I had seen, you pushed your way inside me, and I wept, and my weeping caused you to weep again, and as we made love there in the room by the sea where the sad gray dinghies bobbed and swayed with their masts torn by the wind, and the gulls hovering like angels, and the water spilling and spilling and spilling itself onto the shore, we wept as we each died our little deaths and saw in the simultaneous dark and light of our coming all of who we were together and who we were not apart.

Dear **X**:

   Yes, I see your point. It all sounds banal, reduced to words. Because it is not just sex we are describing, is it? No. It is the thing that we yearn toward through sex, a poignant thing we can never quite attain. Do not call it love. That, we have already, and it is a fine thing but still not enough.

   The coupling of our bodies, the coupling of our hearts is like an exquisite aria as yet unfinished. The ears of our souls strain to hear the final crescendo but falter in the vast incessant silence that follows.

I dream of a dream I dreamt long before I met you but had forgotten among the myriad dreams of people and places I did not recognize:

You were swimming in a calm sea, moving toward shore like a fish grown weary of life in water, choosing in that sudden single-minded moment to evolve into a species that could finally feel the hot sand beneath your feet, and lay down on that sand, and pull down upon you the woman who had walked out of the water so long before that she now feared her desire to be engulfed by it again, but did not fear being engulfed by you— you who still held the essence of water within him.

And then it happened: Your feet touched the sea's floor and you stood and rose from the water, and the water shimmered as it fell from your slick brown skin like electrons finally captured within their nebulous paths.

. . . *and the sun on the water, and the sky on the water, and the water gazing up at the sun and the sky* . . .

New species, I wanted you.

I stood in front of a painting of a man rising out of water, and I said without turning to you, knowing you were near: "See how quickly the water engulfs the absence left by the rising man, as if to battle the sadness of his leaving."

You touched my hair and whispered, "What are the chances?"

I turned to look at you: Your face that close: The path of my blood veered.

Sometimes after you have fallen asleep, I get up and go to the mirror and look at my face to see what it is that makes you want me as you do. I smile at my reflection the way I smile at you, and try to love what I see as you love what you see, thinking it will help me know you better: what you want, what you love, what makes you sigh and tremble.

I make you sigh and tremble!

This, to me, is miraculous.

We roll away from one another and lie on our backs listening to our breaths grow long and deep while outside the wind dissolves to a hesitant breeze and the gulls settle upon the sand to pick at the fruits the sea offers the shore. There is no need to speak now. We have said all we can say with our bodies; the rest we abandon in the futility of words.

Are we happy? Does the gentle ache in our muscles constitute the aftermath of joy?

Before I fall asleep, you give me your hand which I lay over my face to inhale the scent of me on you.

You said, "Shall we go for a walk?"

I nodded, though you knew I knew the question was rhetorical.

Outside the city was clothed in half-darkness, the stars muted, the air bitter with acid vapors of machines. We stood a long while on the pavement staring into the miles of sameness before us: the dim streets, the bitter air, the hidden stars. There was nowhere to walk that would take us out of this landscape which, until now, we had not considered unacceptable. Now it was unacceptable.

"This is unacceptable," you said.

"Yes," I agreed.

"We don't belong here."

"No, not together. Not now."

"One would think that the fact we are here together would lend an air of magic to this city."

"But this city is not magical."

"No, it is hideous."

"Because we're together."

"Precisely for that reason."

A sudden hot wind rose up from the south and tore through the streets like a volatile beast caught in a maze. It growled. It lifted soot and dust and litter and spun it around our heads. Grit stung my cheeks, filled my nose and mouth. I couldn't breathe. I reached out for you, but my hands fell upon nothing. I squinted through the dirty biting wind and saw you stumbling over the pavement, your hands pressed over your eyes. You were screaming: "I can't see! I can't see! My god, I've gone blind!"

Dear **X**:

This is not the time to wake up. You know this. If the dream ends here then you are forever blinded to circumstance, casual or designed. Always, there will be a part of you unable to see what is to occur: the inevitabilities we speak of. Connections between one thing and another will be lost to you, and how can we ever arrive in that room by the sea upon which the sad gray dinghies bob and sway in the wind? What are the gulls but bits of feather and blood and bone if we are not there to make them lovely? Without us, what is the sea itself but a blister upon the flesh of the world?

I need the scent of your fine black hair when it is damp when I kiss it when it falls across my breasts.

Understand me: I need this.

You said, "Shall we go for a walk?"

I shook my head. "I'm sorry, but I'm with someone tonight."

Your face fell hard above your shoulders, and your shoulders hard above your chest, and your chest heaved as you glanced away, then down at your shoes, then at the painting of the woman nude on the bed smiling faintly as if remembering the scent of a man who has just left the room. You continued staring at her as you asked, "This man, does he mean something to you?"

"Something," I said, "but not enough."

You rise from the sea, your fine black hair and slick brown skin shining with wetness, and wade through the shallows onto the shore where the sand folds around your footprints as if to absolve itself of the pleasure of your touch. I watch you move toward me, more than an object of beauty, more than a thing of grace: the exact size and shape of what my soul lacks. You are what I lack. What I have always lacked, even when I was hungry or thirsty or cold. Even when I was not. What I lack.

You move up the beach, smiling at me as I smile at you, our smiles a perfect reflection of each other's: sky and water. The tentative arc between us vanishes in the illusion of who we are together at this moment, in this place, this life.

Are we happy?

You lay yourself down upon the sand and close your eyes and reach your arms up toward the sky and smile. You say: "Fill me with light."

It is not the sun to which you make your demand, but me. And so I place my feet at the side of your ankles and stand gazing down at you who reach toward me, knowing I cannot help but succumb to your desire, for it is my desire to succumb to it.

I will fill you with light.

I spread my body heated by the sun over your body cooled by the water and touch my lips to your lips as I whisper, "I will give you back the light you have given me." And you sigh and collapse your arms over my spine, and part your legs until my legs fall between them, and cover my mouth with your mouth so that I may reach my tongue inside for you to suck on while our groins roll against one another, a tender mimicry of waves upon sand.

The beach is empty. When we remove our clothes, no one protests.

Dear **X**:

How is it we know each other? By our faces, our eyes prematurely locked in recognition? By our voices, their peculiar cadence or timbre? By our scents detected by some primitive synapse hidden so deeply, performing so efficiently that we are not even aware of its function? By our touch —no, that is the last thing we understand.

Then is it simply energy, subatomic particles unbound by space or time that know each other before our faces or voices or scents or hands manifest into the illusion by which we carry ourselves through the world? I knew you before I met you, knew you for years, and thus waited for you to appear exactly as you did: a man with feet polished by sand and hard-soft hips and fine black hairs curling above your trousers toward your navel, your stomach, your slick chest with its tense nipples and pillowy aureolas, your wide shoulders, your thick neck, your face with its palatable lips and aquiline nose and eyes intense and startled when I appeared to you exactly as I did.

"You are exquisite," you said.

Your body the shape of your soul.

I know your soul. And I do not have to see it or hear it or taste it or smell it or touch it to comprehend its exquisite shape.

"This man, does he mean something to you?"

"He is the man who kept me company while I waited for you to appear."

You surveyed the gallery. "Where is he? I want to meet him. I want to thank him for protecting you from loneliness in my absence."

Stay inside me, I can't bear the hollow of your absence.

I grasped you by the elbow and led you through the big white rooms full of paintings. So many rooms! We walked and walked and walked through them, me holding your elbow, you glancing at me each time we passed a man, me shaking my head to say no, that is not him. And then it was him, and I nodded yes, and released your elbow.

You laughed: "What are the chances!"

The man/the artist/your friend/my transitory lover turned toward us, and smiled, and walked up and kissed me on the cheek and then looked at you, his smile waning already, already knowing you were the one I had been waiting for, not he.

How did he know?

He shook your hand and said, "Ah, then. You."

Yes, you. You with your soul shaped like the absence I had carried all these years.

He knew by the absence of absence now filled.

I am still sleeping . . . dreaming of birds upon the shore skittering to and fro against the dance of waves, and the sad gray dinghies suddenly white beneath the sun, their masts raised and full of wind and sailing out to sea, and the sun on the water, and the sky on the water, and the water gazing up at the sun and the sky . . . when you enter me. I do not wake up. Thus, me asleep and you lunging inside me, I dream I am sinking below the waves, and the waves fold around me, and the light through the water is a pale green that grows dark as I sink beneath the sea. I hold my breath, afraid to inhale, fearing the loss of the plea- sure of the scent of the sea that engulfs me drowning in wetness that smells like you and tastes like you, your scent and salt the same as the sea's.

Your voice comes to me from a distance above the waves and the darkening green light. It whispers, "Breathe."

But I am afraid of loss.

It says, "Breathe!"

But I am afraid.

It shouts, "Breathe!"

And I feel your mouth on my mouth, and the wind from your lungs filling my lungs, and sea of your sex filling the cave of my sex, and I come as you come, rising from the depths of dreaming toward the paling green light. Breaking through the surface. My body rocked by the sea's waves, your waves. My face kissed by the wind's mouth, your mouth. My eyes burned by the sun's heat, your heat.

And I wake.

And the dream dissolves.

And I breathe.

Dear **X**:
    Thank you for saving me.

You say, "Thank you."

    . . . *for saving me* . . .

"You're welcome," says the man/the artist/your friend/my transitory lover. "I'm glad you came tonight. And do you like the paintings?"

"Yes," you say. "Especially that one."

The man/the artist/your friend/my transitory lover looks at the painting of the woman nude on the bed smiling faintly as if remembering the scent of a man who has just left the room. "But it is not my scent she remembers," he says as he looks at me. "It never was."

I remember past lovers. None brought me rapture. Before you, rapture was a word; now it is an object.

My time with these men was marked by my hunger for you who hungered for me with a hunger as penetrating as my own. What these men could not give me rises up like a flag of temporal defeat, waving above the landscape of my past, obliterating whatever small pleasures these men had given me in their time. They were so easily sated. Me, never. Even now, when you clutch your hands over my breasts while I squirm upon your lap and my blood converges tight against your converging blood as if straining to amalgamate, your blood and my blood . . . even now, we yearn for what we cannot possibly attain: the exquisite consummation of our souls.

It is this tandem yearning that makes our time together replete with rarefied incidence, our time apart choked with desire.

Dear X:
    I am rarefied. I am choking.

You sleep. I watch you sleeping. I can tell by the smoothness of your brow that your dreams are generous.

You are naked in this borrowed bed. Your body at rest, your soul departed, searching backward through dreams you dreamed of me long before we met.

Where is the beginning of it all?

Find it and let me know.

I stick a finger in my mouth and suck on it. When I do this, do you dream of me?

You moved toward the door and I moved with you, though my body remained behind.

Take my body with you. I have kept it beautiful for you alone.

The man/the artist/your friend/my transitory lover stood beside me, already bent in conversation with a new stranger:

Stranger: "Do you paint from life?"

He: "No, from dreams."

Stranger: "Your dreams, or someone else's?"

He: "What a question!"

I reached inside my purse and removed a square of paper, folded in quarters, yellowed with age and dark along the folds. I went after you and touched your neck where fine black hairs formed a perfect V as you opened the door to leave.

You turned.

I handed you the square of paper and said: "You dropped this."

You unfolded the square of paper and read:

Dear **X**:
    I want you.

And I do: When I remember the past, when I remember the future: the ache between my thighs.

"Come here."
   "Here I am."
   "Closer."
   "This close."
   "Climb upon me."
   "Hold me up."
   "Put your feet here."
   "Put your hands here."
   "Do not close your eyes."
   "My eyes are open."
   "Tell me what you see."
   "I see your need."
   "My desire."
   "Your desire."

"And yours."
"They are the same."
"Precisely the same."

I stand on the whitewashed balcony overlooking the sea. You come up behind me, lift my skirt, press the palms of your hands on my shoulder blades, your mouth against the nape of my neck.

You enter me.

I lean out over the railing, out over the sand below the railing, the gulls upon the sand, the water swirling around the legs of gulls, folding under itself as I fold under you. There is no one to witness our little deaths, to see our bodies lunge toward the tentative arc between sky and water, to hear our voices cry past that arc, O God! except perhaps God—though we beg for witnesses: eyes fixed on the moment.

Dear **X**:

Your point is well taken. We must ignore those who would think us perverse, who would say that what we do naked—and sometimes clothed—is cause for alarm. They are liars. They are afraid. They lie to veil their fear.

We have our desire. We name it then move into it so that it cannot move into us and make us who we are not: a man and a woman hiding from unspeakable desire. We are not.

Do you really think they do not consider making love until their bodies are swollen with fatigue, until sweat oozes from the napes of their necks, streams down their breasts and thighs, dampens even the crevices between their toes, until the painting is loosened from the wall and falls to the floor, until the clean white sheets are stained and torn from the bed, until the high sun sinks behind the tiled rooftops of villas overlooking the ebb and flow of a tide that has made love to the shore so long that the shore no longer regrets what it gives up to the sea nor blushes at what it retrieves from the sea's depths but instead remembers that once it was alone and wounded in its loneliness and now it is healed?

Let's be honest, let's not lie: Our perversions are the vehement choreography of two souls torn apart trying to claw and grapple and writhe their way back together. If we bleed in the process, at least we have each other to lick our wounds.

I stepped out into the night, into the city with its dim streets and bitter air and hidden stars. The man/the artist/your friend/my transitory lover led me down the sidewalk just as a hot wind rose from the south, tearing through the streets like a volatile beast caught in a maze. Grit stung my cheeks, filled my nose and mouth. I couldn't breathe. I reached out and my hands fell upon you who pulled me out of the wind, into an alley that was dark and warm and silent as a womb, a tomb.

You traced my lips with the index finger of your right hand, then slipped the finger between my lips and pried them open. You leaned close. I could feel your breath, smell its scent of warm milk. You kissed me—O *do not underestimate the weight of a kiss*—your mouth like a ripe mango split open beneath an exotic sun, its heart slick and sweet and wet, its core a temperate hollow begging to be filled. I filled it with my tongue, my teeth, my lips. I immersed myself inside you—what you expected, what you wanted. You moaned and drew me close and lifted my skirt and slid your hands over my naked bottom, always naked, waiting for this moment, your hands. You pulled me tight against you, and I could feel your hardness and wanted it inside me, inside my own temperate hollow . . .

. . . *which is where you want to be, and so you lift me up by my bottom and I wrap my legs around your waist and cling to your neck while you press my back against the blood-red bricks of the alley wall, and kiss me wet and hard, and reach between my legs to unzip your trousers. They fall to the pavement . . .*

> Dear **X**:
> No, not here. This is not the place or the time. You know the place: a white room with two doors that open onto a balcony that looks out upon a sea where the sad gray dinghies bob and sway. And as for the time? We will know it when we get there, knowing now that we may have already arrived.

. . . my back against the blood-red bricks of the alley wall as you reach between my legs to unzip your trousers, then stop, and pull your mouth away from my mouth and look at me, at my eyes dilated with questionable assent as you whisper:

"Not here."

"No, not here."

Beyond the alley, the man/the artist/your friend/my transitory lover stumbles over the pavement, hands pressed over his eyes, screaming: "I can't see! I can't see! My god, I've gone blind!"

We wake on sand to find ourselves surrounded by hundreds of seagulls, their legs like yellow twigs sprung from dry earth. They do not look at us but stare out to sea, past the tentative arc that separates sky from water, water from sky.

The gulls are silent and still, as if listening.

What is it they hear? What is it they see? Have our dreams washed through them like waves through sand? Are they therefore changed by our vision of each other—you and I, asleep or awake? Vicarious participants in our desire, does their consciousness now seek to evolve into who we are, as we seek to evolve into who we are not? Not yet us: a man and a woman with interchangeable dreams.

The gulls stare beyond the tentative arc between water and sky. The wind purls their feathers.

None of this has happened.

This is one theory, and how can we refute it? We have no evidence, no witnesses. The salt of your neck on my tongue, the scent of my sex on your hand—these prove nothing to no one. No one but us. And even to us they prove nothing but our longing to heal the wound of our souls.

Our souls: torn apart. Our bodies: clawing, grappling, writhing.

What greater tragedy than unquenchable desire? What lesser hope than doubted possibilities?

Dear **X**:

What is perversion but the inability to comprehend?

Dear **X**:
  We comprehend.

I wake to find myself inside your dream: a white room. An unrumpled bed. A painting on the wall of a woman smiling faintly as if remembering the scent of a man who has just left the room. And you—having just left the room—stand on the whitewashed balcony overlooking the sea.

A cigarette burns close to your knuckles. A gull hovers at your periphery. You flick the cigarette over the chalky railing onto the sand below. You run a hand through your fine black hair the way it smells when it is damp when I kiss it when it falls across my breasts.

You turn.

And for a moment you do not see me as you enter the room, your dream, but see still the vision that fastened your eyes to the horizon. Then it vanishes: the vision, the horizon. And you halt as if startled.

You say: "You're here."

There is a moment—eternal, inexistent—when we do not speak, unable to find words to fill the moment with what we know the moment to be, have known it to be always, before we were, before the particles of who we are came together to make us who we are, particles knowing each other before we knew ourselves, each other: the waves throbbing upon the shore, the gulls reeling over rooftops, the dinghies suddenly white with their masts raised full of wind and moving out to sea beyond the tentative arc of line that separates water from sky.

Dear **X**:
  Here I am: water.

Dear **X**:
  There you are: sky.

With your soul shaped like the absence I carry, of which I now unburden myself as I unbutton your trousers that . . . *your exquisite soul, inscrutable and intense, the precise shape of your body* . . . fall to the floor.

Has none of this happened? Do you not exist?

My testament: I want you more now than when I began, as if I once had you completely then lost you among this ruin of words.

Therefore: It has all happened.

It is happening now.

And now.

And now.

And now . . .

Chairman of the Board

HE SAID, "Goddamn it, drive!"

"I gotta red light in front of me."

"I don't care if you've got the entire Red Army in front of you, I have a board meeting in twenty minutes and I want to be moving forward *now!*"

"Yes, sir. Okay, sir."

The limousine pulled into the intersection just as a white Pontiac traveling 40 MPH entered from the west. The driver of the Pontiac did not brake before impact, thus the limousine was bent into a nearly perfect arc, the left side curving deeply inward against the right.

When the noise of metal and glass had quieted, and the angle of the sun had settled into a solitary direction, he heard "O madre santa o hijo de puta!" screamed repeatedly in a rhythmic falsetto which at first he mistook for a song on the radio, then recognized as the driver's voice when he also heard, beneath the screaming, the aria from Donizetti's *Lucia di Lammermoor.* He hated Donizetti but considered the screaming much more cacophonous and so ordered the driver to shut the hell up. It seemed, however, that his voice did not move beyond the confines of his skull, and the driver continued screaming.

At the time of the accident he had been approximately seven minutes late. Now he attempted to look at his watch in

order to determine the extent to which his day had been dis-
rupted. But no hand moved to his face. In fact, he could not
discern the exact location of his left arm. Neither could he
locate his right arm or his legs. When he tried to summon a
limb into his line of vision, it was as if his thoughts slid to the
base of his skull, slithered along the gray fibers of his hair, then
quickly dissipated into the stifling atmosphere.

Briefly he panicked. He struggled to raise himself into a vertical position, although he could not be certain that his body
lay horizontally since the sunlight filtered toward him through
a maze of fabric, glass, and metal. When he detected the hot
thick sickeningly sweet odor of blood and what he concluded
to be his own excrement, he immediately ceased struggling and
began to wait.

Thus:

In the instant before his death he recalls the year 1952 and
himself as a young man standing in the small square backyard of
the house on Langley Street, watering the young hedges with a
new garden hose, the morning light trembling against the red-
dening leaves of a maple growing up through the white fence, a
bright yellow finch hopping from one picket spire to the next,
the neighbor's obese tomcat crouching among the marigolds and
emitting an odd sort of *ba-a-a* as it slowly whipped its tail from
side to side, its eyes tracking the finch's course. Recalls the sound
of lawn mowers, near and distant, a small-engine plane passing
overhead, a barking dog, his son's tiny voice shouting, "Daddy,
look, look, look! Look *here!*" Recalls twisting the spigot until the
garden hose went limp, wiping his hands on his cotton shorts,
walking to the edge of the small vegetable garden planted by his
first wife—a woman who liked the scent of dirt and leaves.
Recalls the garden's edge where his son, towheaded and already
brown from summer, squatted in front of a metal garden stake,
aiming a miniature finger at it and repeating, "Look, look, look!"
Recalls squinting just beyond the boy's finger, above it and to the
left, and witnessing a shiny black ant struggling to carry a moth's

wing up the stake, succeeding halfway to the top, then falling to the ground, then grasping again the gray-brown dusty wing and again attempting the impossible ascent, then falling again, ascending again, falling. . . . Recalls the sound of his own voice, a voice remarkably cheerful and young and confident as it concluded, "Silly old ant." Recalls, finally, his son standing and curling his hands into little fists and positioning them on his hips and shaking his golden head in disdain as he repeated with perfect mimicry, "Silly old ant. Silly, *silly* old ant!"

And it is precisely there, at that peculiar intimate immeasurably fractious moment between living and not living, when he hears the driver's screaming abruptly cease and thinks: *What an odd thing to remember. At a time like this.*

Pavlov's Smile

WHEN MARCELO MOVED out of the house, Vera let his dog sleep in her bed, but it wasn't the same: The dog shed. And when she dreamed of floods or fires or crashing planes and drew the animal to her breasts, it whined pitifully, spinning its tiny legs like a garden tiller. Too often she woke with stiff hairs matted in her eyes and short pink scratches marring the paper-white flesh of her arms. The morning after the dog drew blood, she called Arturo.

Arturo was not Marcelo's best friend. No, he was not a friend at all. He was, however, from Argentina, as was Marcelo. Thus, the two men tolerated what they considered to be the other's inadequacies for the sake of a lingering patriotism. Arturo envied Marcelo's excessive good looks and despised his excessive dishonesty. Marcelo feared Arturo's immoderate intelligence and loathed his immoderate self-righteousness. But when Marcelo and Arturo met on the street, they smiled and shook hands and talked about Argentina with a mutually heartsick nostalgia.

Three months earlier, Marcelo had introduced Vera to Arturo. She had liked him well enough, had even desired him, briefly, for no more than an instant, when she'd seen the good white teeth, the lucid eyes, the strong brown legs. Then she had remembered her monogamy—that persistent onus—and the desire had dissipated like a premature fog.

Although Arturo was almost a stranger, Vera now decided he would make a good lover. She recalled how he'd taken her hand between his palms, pressed it once and firmly, and then slowly slid the palms off and away. She recalled how the muscles of his legs and arms had flexed involuntarily while he spoke, as if releasing particles of sexual energy which his youth, though retreating, could not wholly contain. More importantly, she recalled his lucid eyes: how they rolled over her body like two stones—cool, indifferent, yet somehow lustful.

Vera propped the phone between her ear and shoulder, set the dog on the floor, and dialed. The phone rang and rang. The dog hopped for a moment on its hind legs, then put its front paws on Vera's knees and whined. She kicked it away. "Go! You had your chance."

The dog slowly backed away, sat on its hindquarters and ducked its head.

Immediately remorseful, Vera stretched her free hand toward the animal. "Oh, I'm sorry, my perrito! Please come here. Please!"

The dog yelped and scuttled beneath the bed.

As Vera was about to hang up, Arturo answered. His voice was broken and gravelly like an old recording. It was three o'clock in the morning. Vera knew he had been asleep but did not bother to apologize. Instead, she came straight to the point. "Would you like to take me to a movie tomorrow evening?"

"Yes, of course," yawned Arturo. "Who is this?"

"Vera."

"Vera who?"

"Vera, Marcelo's girlfriend."

"Ah, yes. How is the chanta, anyway?"

"Gone."

"Gone?"

"He left me two weeks ago."

"What a tragedy," Arturo said flatly. "Which movie would you like to see?"

They went to a theater in the southern barrio which showed only films of violence and war. The movie was not one which Vera would have selected, but she had not been able to make up her mind and so had let Arturo decide. Arturo drove a motorcycle too fast, drank mint tea spiked with bourbon and was studying (at a leisurely pace) to be a doctor of psychology. Vera guessed it was this combination which accounted for his taste in movies.

Before the lights went down, Vera presented Arturo with an abbreviated account of Marcelo's departure: "We were walking on the plaza. I caught him staring at young girls in their thin summer dresses. His eyes watered. I told him, *If you are going to become so emotional about girls in summer dresses, then maybe you should be chasing after them, hmm?* When we returned home, he began packing his things. I asked him where he was going. He told me, *To chase girls in summer dresses.*"

She bit into a hangnail.

"And that was all?" asked Arturo.

"Yes."

He studied her for a moment, then shrugged his shoulders. "He will come back."

She spit out the hangnail. "Who cares."

The movie began.

Vera drew her knees up against her chest and slid down in her seat. At the first hint of bloodshed, she pressed her forehead to her kneecaps and closed her eyes. Immediately after she did this, Arturo said, "A-a-a-a-a!" and laughed maniacally. He was not laughing at her; he was laughing at the movie. The more violent the scene, the louder Arturo laughed. People stared. Vera stared, too, then announced, "You're crazy."

Arturo raised one eyebrow. "Laughter is a perfectly healthy way to relieve anxiety."

"Ah, sure it is." She went to the bathroom and did not come out until the movie was nearly over.

Arturo drove his motorcycle across Vera's front lawn and onto her veranda. She stumbled off the back, quickly removed her helmet and threw it at Arturo, who deftly caught it with one hand.

"I'm a nervous wreck!" she shouted.

Arturo cut the engine. "As I advised, you should have laughed."

"I'm not talking about the lousy movie. I'm talking about your lousy driving."

"What's wrong with my driving?"

"Too fast. Too reckless. Just look!" She indicated the fine red dust adorning her calves like unimaginative tattoos. "My legs brushed up against *cars!*"

"I know what I'm doing."

"Sure you do."

She spun around and unlocked the front door.

Arturo sat on his motorcycle. He did not remove his helmet but stared at a white moth beating its powdery wings against the street lamp. His hands clutched and twisted the handle grips as if he were still maneuvering through traffic.

Vera put her hands on her hips. "Well? Are you coming in or not?"

Arturo looked up at the night sky. He studied the moon, then Orion, then searched for the North Star. "I think perhaps I should go home," he said coolly. "There are moments when one's psyche isn't suited to the company of others. When one knows one's present temperament dictates that one will do or say something inappropriate, something one will eventually regret."

"In other words, you're angry because I criticized your driving."

Arturo gave a couple of violent twists to the handle grips. "Precisely."

Vera said, "Grow up and be a man," and went inside.

As she was undressing for bed, she heard Arturo's motorcycle drive off very fast into the night.

Vera sat in the bathtub until the flesh of her hands and feet wrinkled. She scooped the last ice cube from the water's surface and slid it over her face. Then she ran the tips of her fingers over her breasts, hummed a very old tune and thought of Marcelo.

Specifically, she recalled an evening when she had stood at the kitchen counter chopping vegetables for a salad. She had been wearing a tank top, a thin cotton skirt, and nothing beneath. Marcelo had sat smoking a cigarette at the kitchen table, watching her hands as they maneuvered the vegetables into place before brutally attacking them. He had slowly stood, crushed the cigarette into the ashtray, walked up behind her, and lifted her skirt. He had run his hands over her round white bottom, set his chin onto her shoulder and whispered, "Don't stop cutting." She didn't. Not even when she felt him enter her. Not even when the knife sliced off a thin sliver of her left index finger.

Now, she lifted the wet wrinkled finger and looked at the old scar. She sucked on it and wept.

Outside it was summer. The air was unbearably hot and humid. Buildings, trees, and automobiles stood heavy on the pavement as if temperature had weight. People waded through the shimmering heat waves rising from the plaza; they squinted up at the blue-white sky; they dabbed at the sweat above their lips, complaining, always complaining. Ordinary women became more ordinary, flowers wilted, birds sang less.

Alone in his room, he listened to the hot silence and wiped the sweat from his eyes with a towel. He counted the number of flies on the yellow coil of paper hanging from the naked light bulb. He drank four glasses of iced mint tea and bourbon. He called Vera.

"How have you been?"

"Very well, thank you. Who is this?"

"Arturo."

"Oh. Arturo."

Vera stood naked in the middle of her living room, elbows positioned away from her body, legs set apart. The window fan inhaled the hot outer air, exhaled it into the room and dried the bathwater from her skin.

"Do you have air conditioning?" Arturo asked.

"No."

"But you have trees."

"Trees?"

"In your yard there are trees."

"Yes."

"Then I would like to visit you."

"Why?"

"Because my apartment is very hot."

"And? What else?"

Arturo paused in irritation; he did not wish to state the obvious for it would provide him no psychological escape should he be rejected. He considered hanging up but a new stream of sweat trickled down his forehead, passed through the furrow between his brows and veered into his left eye. He winced and said unhappily, "Because I would like to see you."

"Okay, but come soon. Before I change my mind."

She hung up the phone and put her hands on her hips. The dog *tick-tick-ticked* across the wooden floor and, panting miserably, looked up at her. She held out her hands in supplication. "So, what did you expect me to tell him, hm?"

She met Arturo at the front door wearing nothing but a man's white shirt buttoned halfway. Arturo stared at the glistening crevice between her breasts, and when she turned and led him into the living room, he stared at the glistening spheres of her buttocks swaying beneath the shirttail.

"What a nice shirt," he told her.

"Yes, Marcelo left it." She pressed her face against the sleeve, closed her eyes and inhaled. "It still smells like him."

Arturo's mouth jerked open, then shut.

They sat down, Arturo on a stiff wooden chair and Vera on the couch with her legs crossed beneath her. They looked at each other. Arturo tapped the wooden arm of the chair with the back of his ring. Vera drummed the fingers of one hand against her thigh; her other hand slid from the back of her neck to the front, then down between her breasts, attempting to wipe away the gathering sweat but instead moving it from one heated spot to the next.

"So. What do you think?"

"I think," Arturo said carefully, "this is a seduction."

Vera's expression did not change except for a brief and slight rise at one corner of her mouth. "Well, someone has to do it. You. Or me. I prefer it be me."

Arturo stood to approach her, but she shook her head and pointed through the door toward the bedroom. After a brief hesitation, he went in and sat on the edge of the bed, waiting.

A moment later, Vera stood naked in the doorway, staring down at him. "It's been over five years since I've made love to anyone except Marcelo."

"I understand."

"No," she said, moving toward him, "I doubt that you do."

During sex Vera said *Marcelo* twice. Each time, Arturo winced. When Vera climbed on top of him and her breaths grew long and deep, he said, "Say my name." She looked down at him and narrowed her eyes. He repeated, "Say my name." She clamped her teeth together and thrust her pelvis forward with greater ferocity. "Say my name, Vera." As she climaxed, she screamed, "No!"

Afterward, as Vera lay facedown on the bed, Arturo slid a hand over the sweat on the small of her back. "Actually, it's not surprising that you would call me Marcelo."

"Oh, really?" yawned Vera.

"Are you familiar with Pavlov's dog?"

"Yes."

"Well, then, you must agree that this situation is quite a bit like that one. Pavlov rings a bell each time he feeds his dog. The dog salivates when he hears the bell because it associates the ringing with food. A conditioned response."

"Mm."

"You make love with the same man for five years. You asso-
ciate him with sex. Therefore, when you make love now you
say *Marcelo*. A conditioned response." He paused and brushed a
damp strand of hair away from Vera's face. Her eyes were closed.
"It's very much the same," he added unnecessarily. Then he put
a hand on her shoulder and gently shook it. "Vera? Are you
awake?"

She said nothing.

He laid his head back against the pillow. "It's quite possible
that I like you, Vera. It's certain that I hate Marcelo."

"He hates you, too," Vera mumbled, then rolled toward Marcelo, pressing the length of her whiteness against the length of
his brownness. "And as for Pavlov," she said, "I'm sure he felt
terribly smug when the dog drooled. I'm sure it pleased him.
I'm sure he smiled. The bastard."

Arturo lay perfectly still, waiting for her to continue. By the
time he raised his head to look at her, she was truly asleep.

Every night for the next two months, Arturo drove his motorcycle onto Vera's veranda, went inside her house, and made love
to her. Vera did not mention Marcelo's name again except to
say, once, that his white shirt now smelled only of her perfume.
Arturo had nodded, wrung his hands, and grinned.

One evening after they had made love three times, pausing
only momentarily before beginning again, Arturo kissed a small
wet salty river flowing between Vera's breasts and said, "Perhaps
I'm not in love with you, Vera, but I like you very much, and I
think that might be good."

Vera had looked at him hard and said, "You fill a void."

At the end of summer, on a late morning after the first cool
rain, Arturo was walking through the plaza when he ran into
Marcelo. The two men smiled at each other and shook hands.
They did not talk about Argentina.

"So," smiled Marcelo, "there is a rumor that you've been sleeping with Vera."

Arturo nodded, aware that his own labored smile was not as handsome as Marcelo's, neither as practiced nor as buoyant—a buoyancy which seemed to make Marcelo's perfectly proportioned body levitate two or three inches above the earth, causing him to appear taller, stronger, superior. Arturo instinctively pulled his shoulders back and nodded. "The rumor is true."

Marcelo stuck out his lower lip, then sucked it in. "How is she, anyway?"

"Quite well."

"Good. That's good."

"We may move in together."

"Ah, really?"

"Yes. It was Vera's suggestion."

"It would be a mistake."

"A mistake for whom?"

Marcelo's gaze wandered across the street to where two young women were giggling in front of a shop window. He sighed wistfully, then turned back to Arturo. "For Vera."

"She doesn't love you, Marcelo."

"She wouldn't tell you if she did."

"What the hell do you know, anyway?"

"I lived with Vera for five years. I know a lot."

Arturo shifted his feet as if regaining his balance. He pressed a hand firmly against his temple to stop the pounding there. "I must go. Vera and I are meeting for dinner."

"How lovely!" said Marcelo, extending his hand to Arturo.

Arturo hesitated, then reciprocated.

Marcelo smiled. "Ciao, my friend."

"Sure. Ciao."

As Arturo walked away he heard Marcelo call after him, "You will tell Vera you saw me, won't you?"

Arturo kept walking, pretending not to hear.

———

Between the soup and salad, Arturo began laughing maniacally. Vera smoked a cigarette and stared at him, slowly blinking her eyes. When his laughter had subsided and he had wiped the tears from his face, he chuckled, "Well, you can't guess who I ran into today."

"Marcelo."

"How did you know?"

"He told me."

"When?"

"Tonight. On the phone. He called just before you arrived."

Arturo's left eye twitched.

Vera tapped her cigarette over the ashtray. The waiter brought the salad. She looked down at it, then back at Arturo. "I'm not hungry."

Arturo leaned toward her and narrowed his eyes. "But are you in love?"

"With whom?"

"With Marcelo."

"I think of him often."

"While we're making love?"

"Yes."

"But you no longer say his name."

"I say it. You don't hear me."

Arturo clutched the sides of the table. "You asked me to move in with you."

"I don't like sleeping alone."

"Do you like sleeping with me?"

"Yes." She put her chin in her hand and said wearily, "But it's not the same."

When Arturo drove his motorcycle onto the veranda, Vera climbed off and slowly removed her helmet. Arturo reached for it. She tucked it beneath her arm. "Are you coming in?"

He looked at her face which was white in the moonlight. Then he shook his head and looked at the moon. "I don't understand you, Vera."

"I never apologize for emotions."

"Marcelo is a liar. He will leave you again."

"Yes, I know."

"Will you call me after he goes?"

"Yes."

She held the helmet toward him. He took it. She unlocked the front door. "You're sure you won't come in?"

"I'm sure."

Vera stepped toward him and lightly kissed his cheek. He grabbed the nape of her neck, drew her mouth to his and buried his tongue inside. Then he pushed her away. Vera stared at him a moment, turned, and went into the house.

Arturo twisted the handle grips. He looked up at the moon. He laughed.

For a long while, Vera stood at her bedroom window listening for the sound of Arturo's motorcycle tearing off into the night. There was silence. Finally she heard the engine rev once, heard the rumbling move out across her lawn and then, very slowly, disappear down the street. She sighed.

She let the curtains fall back into place and lay down on the bed. Marcelo's dog jumped onto her stomach and began licking her cheek. She pulled it gently to her and rolled over onto her side. The dog began to whine and fight against her embrace. She drew it closer and tighter against her breasts. The dog drew blood. She whispered, "Hush, hush, hush, hush . . ."

She stared at the phone. She waited for it to ring.

Prayers Of An Accidental Nature

WE DID NOT know Claudia well. In truth, we did not know her at all. Her dossier, so to speak, was a thin one padded primarily with information we had extracted from Samuel. The remaining data were mere speculation based on the style of her shoes, the cut of her skirt, her argot, and, yes, her appetite for bad cuisine.

Up until that evening—that singular moment when she spoke out with such startling confidence for a girl her age and (speculated) background—until that very moment, what we remembered above all else was Samuel's first vision of her: a small gracefully boned young woman squatting on the dewy verdant lawn of the art museum, long blue-black hair tucked behind her ears, brown tapered fingers of one hand sifting through grass while the other clutched a mason jar half-full of black dirt and— we still shudder to imagine it—*earthworms!*

Of course Samuel's version was longer, romanticized, laden with delicate adjectives and complex metaphors. Dear, young Samuel! Samuel: who once wished to be poet but was gingerly (well, perhaps not so gingerly) dissuaded from such an impractical occupation by his father, a banker. Samuel, who is now vice president of one of his father's smaller, less conspicuous banks, one in which (rumor has it) he spends an inordinate amount of time staring out of the high windows of his office and sighing.

Still, how we love him! Our Samuel: young, handsome, rich! He is like our own prodigal son. Although we sometimes wonder what will become of him, wonder about his fruitless sighs, his taste in music, literature, women . . .

For example: Claudia.

That evening in autumn. The lightless light. The dead ashes on the gray stone hearth. Claudia's voice—fragile and euphonic—competing against the howling wind.

We had just finished a perfectly fine dinner of roast duck, saffron rice, and honey-dilled baby carrots in a mustard glaze.

But wait!

Perhaps we should choose our words more carefully. Perhaps we should not use the word *perfectly* at all, though we have in the past inserted it (and variations thereof) into conversations and correspondence with great frequency. Omit especially now the word *perfectly* because those honey-dilled baby carrots in a mustard glaze tasted very much the way canned garden vegetables smell after they've been overcooked and tossed into a metal garbage can upon which the summer sun beats inexorably down for a full week, at which point you step outside your back door, stare up at the hot sun (automatically wiping your brow though you are not yet perspiring) and, made curious by the strange aroma coming from inside the can, you lift the metal lid. . . . Yes, that simultaneously sweet and putrid odor which results. A stench of death and rot.

Even so, everyone ate the carrots, chewing them slowly, hesitantly, smiling and nodding at Evelyn (Mrs George) Wilton, our hostess/cook, as rich as when George was alive (perhaps richer) but still stubbornly insistent upon preparing dinner parties with her own hands, flaunting the residue of her middle-class past. *Middle-class* before George bought up half the prime real estate in the city, before Evelyn even had the option of hiring a caterer—years ago, when she herself cooked and cleaned, experimenting with new waxes and detergents and scouring powders, testing new recipes clipped from the back of ordinary women's magazines, receiving, as it were, a self-appointed degree in domesticity of which she was and still is (sad to say) extremely proud.

Thus, dinner cooked by Evelyn's own (liver-spotted) hands. And we, nodding and smiling at her as she studied our reactions with discrete worry (as well she should have worried!). We, raising our eyebrows toward her end of the long mahogany table and humming in unison a falsetto, "M-m-m-m!" just before swallowing (with supreme difficulty) those dreadful carrots and then dabbing the corners of our eyes with her fine linen napkins. Our eyes: weeping, as it were, from disgust.

Except Samuel. Samuel, who obviously valued his life above etiquette, did not eat the carrots but instead cut them into thin slivers and tucked a few beneath his naked duck bones, cleverly moving the rest around his plate so as to give the appearance of at least partial consumption.

Oh, and Claudia, who ate the carrots with such hearty speed that it became frightfully evident she actually *enjoyed* their flavor. Either that or she was famished. (Claudia was half Peruvian or Bolivian—we cannot remember which. Her mother was not from the wealthy minority of South Americans, the unordained nobility. Not like Dr Eduardo Martinez, the famous psychiatrist whom we all admire and respect even though his skin is awfully dark, even in winter. No. As we recall from our conversations with Samuel, Claudia's mother was extremely poor and possibly Indian—Incan or Mayan or the like—from a tiny remote village in the Andes.) And since we do not know a thing about her father except that he was American—*North* American, thank god!—it's possible that Claudia was famished, *literally,* rather than devoid of discriminating taste (buds). Although we couldn't imagine Samuel not feeding the girl, what with that awkwardly generous heart of his.

In any event.

Dinner at Evelyn's: not perfectly fine. Simply fine. Fine enough. As dinners at Evelyn's go.

Afterward we retreated (we do not use the verb lightly) into Evelyn's living room which had been newly redecorated, now smelling of paint and varnish and fabric dyes. Beyond the French doors we could see her rather immodest fountain (which she willfully refers to as a birdbath, to which we sardonically respond, "A bath for emus, maybe!"). Her fountain: slowly filling with the sad bronze and copper leaves of autumn, the water rising up, falling down, pounding against the leaves and shattering them into striking resemblances of polished and rusted shrapnel.

The wind moaned against the French doors. Inside, a barbarous fire caused the damp logs to snap and pop and spew tiny sparks onto the stone hearth. We cautiously watched the sparks leap as we drank extremely good brandy and smoked extremely good cigars—only the men of course smoking—all of them except Samuel, who does not smoke cigars no matter how expensive or rare, does not in fact smoke anything at all, not since graduate school (Harvard, of course) when he accidentally smoked a marijuana cigarette laced with opium or heroin or some other dastardly Asian drug and subsequently became quite ill. Was in fact hospitalized for a few days after having seen, he said, "the hideous mask of death and the vast emptiness it disguised." (Such a romantic!) Not wishing, he said, to repeat the experience until no other option exists, which he hopes shall not be for fifty-plus years. (Samuel is much younger than us. Certainly more liberal, more adventurous, less *private*. We have never smoked marijuana—or if we have will never admit to it, not even on our deathbeds which will likely be turned down, our mortal pillows fluffed, long before Samuel's. That is the way we are: growing old. Our secrets, at least, still intact.)

We sipped brandy. The sparks died into bits of ash on the gray stone. We watched their tiny deaths with solemn interest, trying to discern if there existed a significance within their tragic little performances—all of us watching and discerning—all of us except Chas who must have been reflecting upon those damned baby carrots (no doubt wondering how it was possible that a man with a portfolio as plump as his should have to suffer through such a culinary disaster when poor Ethiopians, though starving to death, did not), for he suddenly cleared his throat and, taking a single step toward the center of the room, announced in his solid baritone: "It is most assuredly an imperfect world!"

We looked at him a moment, uncertain as to whether we should smile or wrinkle our brows—and so, to be safe, smiling *and* wrinkling in anticipation of a preface to his seemingly unarguable conclusion which he had surely (we thought) considered before engaging his vocal chords since he is not the sort to burst forth with non sequiturs or empty resolutions, *exempli gratia,* being the successful and highly regarded trial lawyer he is.

It may have been, however, a rare evening for him, the honey-dilled baby carrots in a mustard glaze adversely affecting his mental constitution, for he did not utter another word. Not a single, justifying word. And we, finally realizing this disconcerting fact (our smiles abandoning our wrinkled brows, our brows wrinkling slightly more), we felt embarrassed for our good friend Chas, thinking to ourselves: *How old he has grown these past few years!* Wondering if there is a correlation between the burgeoning number of gray hairs on his head and this first, as far as we knew, incident of senility. And wondering, too, how long before our own incident. And would we even know it when it arrived? And had it already arrived, unbeknownst to us?

Embarrassed, trapped within the silence Chas left hanging in the air alongside the blue-gray smoke of cigars, we nodded our heads slowly, raised our brandies to our lips (our fingers trembling just a bit), and looked away—away from Chas, at one another, passing meaningful glances over the rims of our snifters as we helped ourselves to uncharacteristically impolite gulps of Evelyn's very good brandy.

The red sparks flung themselves onto the gray stone. And died.

Now we must consider the perplexing matter of time:

How it can seem to move so quickly and yet so slowly, too. How, as in the former case, the period between one summer and the next now seems like a common finch flown onto the lawn and then off again while our heads were turned only briefly away, though in reality 365 days (365 finches) have come and gone.

Consider how, in the latter case, the period between Chas's solitary edict, "It is most assuredly an imperfect world!" and our impolite gulps of brandy (less a commentary than a defense) seemed nearly an eternity, though in reality *not more than one minute had passed*.

The perplexing matter of time.

In consideration thereof:

The successive moment was not terribly delinquent when Claudia, who stood by the French doors which were slightly ajar so as to let some of the cigar smoke out and the autumn air in, turned slowly around and lowered her untouched glass of brandy and replied confidently and (we must admit) kindly, not only to Chas but to all of us:

"No. It is a perfect world. And I have seen its perfection."

Claudia.

We truly did not know her at all, had not met her before that evening, though Samuel had been seeing her for over three months.

"A secret affair!" we chided him.

He insisted there was nothing secret about it at all.

To which we enthusiastically replied, "Then why don't you invite her to dinner one of these evenings?"

To which he replied without enthusiasm, "Well . . . perhaps I will. One of these evenings."

In the meantime, we conspired to get Samuel drunk and pry out as much history of the girl as possible without bringing about the boy's untimely (is it ever timely?) demise.

He had been, he said, out for his usual predawn run. (Samuel does not *jog*. He is a remarkable athlete even now, though he drinks quite a lot more than he used to and is consequently beginning to plump above the belt. In prep school he made the All-American soccer team and was offered a full athletic scholarship to UCLA which he declined, preferring instead to concentrate wholly on his studies at Yale. *Yale:* where some dreadful untenured academic led him away from economics and into the black hole of creative writing—*poetry*, no less! —from which he did not emerge until his father, shrewd man that he is, helped him see the pragmatism of a Harvard MBA. *Harvard:* where Samuel learned it was indeed possible to run ten miles a day and still graduate with honors, and hence has not stopped running. Although we quietly wonder among ourselves when he will begin putting those honors to the test.)

"Thus," he told us, slumped in his father's worn Chippendale wing chair, the oxblood leather and surplus wine giving his pale flawless skin a heartier glow, "thus the sky rising with light, resembling a sheet of unpolished steel as my particular though shifting spot of the world rotated toward the sun. And I, running my usual route through quiet neighborhoods that were beginning to hiss with water sprinklers, along the grassy median between empty boulevards, past the tall red-brick condominiums and onto the sidewalk skirting the museum's vast low-clipped lawn . . . seeing first an ordinary hallucination, an imaginary love, a sexual wish, and then realizing with an astonishment that caused me to stumble . . . realizing she was as real and tangible as I. Perhaps more so!"

He smiled seductively to himself, causing not a few of us to blush. Then he announced: "Claudia! Squatting like an Indian goddess of ancient myth! Sifting through the grass! Plucking from it a long pink earthworm writhing with anguish in the lightless light of predawn!"

"Earthworms!" we exclaimed, sputtering nervous chuckles, suppressing giggles, shuddering with repulsion. "What in the name of heaven *for?*"

And Samuel—looking from one face to the next, astounded by our ignorance—said, "Why, for fishing, of course!"

But, you see, he had built up the story so, transformed a common girl gathering earthworms into, as he himself would have paraphrased: *a goddess imbued with magic of mythical proportions.* Somewhere within our vaults of diverse, convenient trivia, we knew earthworms were sometimes used for fishing. Though none of us had ever fished with anything but beautiful hand-wrought lures—or in any event would never admit to having fished with anything else. Yet to gather such creatures from the dew! To actually touch them, feel their loathsome coldness, their subordinate writhing . . . *well!* We could only imagine it, briefly, before turning our minds away from its horror.

Samuel finished off his sixth glass of port. We handed him another. He took it absently, staring past us at some unseen object in the center of the room. Then he slowly began to rise from his chair, speaking with such a hushed voice that we found it necessary to lean toward him and hold our breaths.

"I approached her slowly," he whispered as he moved stealthily toward the center of the room, "slowly . . . slowly . . . fearing she might vanish if I approached too quickly. My breath grew rapid but not from the run. I'd traveled only five miles, after all, a mere third of my regular route. No, my shortness of breath was caused by her . . . her *glorious beauty,* the miracle of it, emanating from her like a . . . *a sun of heaven.* Warmer, more brilliant, more *life-giving* than the now ordinary sun of our planet. Our sadly common sun. Which just then began to shyly present itself above the jagged horizon, obviously humbled by Claudia's *ethereal light.*"

He stood now in the center of the room, staring down at a mauve rose woven within the woolen rug yet seeing (we were certain) a flower much lovelier. Certainly more fragrant since the one before us was, after all, simply a rose woven of wool.

He took a deep gulp of wine, causing us to simultaneously wince and rejoice—wince because the gulp was audible; rejoice because we knew it was bound to loosen his tongue even more. (We ourselves were growing a bit drunk, having had to consume more wine than we were accustomed to in order to coax Samuel toward helpless inebriation.) As he lowered his glass, his tall remarkably taut (as we now wistfully recall) body staggered ever so slightly. We gasped, reaching toward him, the movement of our hands resembling the impeccable choreography of underwater flora—carnivorous flora reaching for the nescient fish—reaching out and immediately withdrawing as he held up a steady hand and replanted his feet on the rug. We relaxed our shoulders and sighed.

"I asked her what," said Samuel, leaning forward and downward over the woolen rose, "what . . . *What are you looking for?* And she looked up at me, already smiling. Smiling, I tell you! Can you imagine?"

Truthful, we shook our heads no.

"I could have been a rapist," he said. "Perhaps a murderer, a monster of a man, bent on unspeakable violence—"

Some of us gasped, "Oh!"

"But she saw me and knew right away, before even looking into my eyes. She knew . . . she knew . . . What did she know?"

He straightened himself up, glanced around the room at each of us, one by one, and repeated, like a professor to daft students: "What did she know?" Then he finished off his wine, set his glass on a lovely English walnut table, spread his arms out wide into the room and laughed, "My God, *everything!*"

We stared at him.

He laughed again. "It's true! She knew absolutely everything about me!"

We stared at each other in bewilderment, then looked once again at Samuel, trying to comprehend his meaning by studying his outspread arms, his broad-grinning mouth, his blue (oh, *painfully* blue!) eyes which, though silently pleading for our erudition, offered us not a single clue in return.

Suddenly he raised a hand to his temple, let it slide down his cheek until it rested on his lips, and dropped heavily to his knees onto the rug, swaying there for a moment before falling the rest of the way. We swooped down around him, taking his hand in ours, brushing his auburn hair from his pale, pale forehead, loosening his tie, bending low to his ear, whispering, "Please, tell us, Samuel—"

"—yes, tell us—"

"—how could she have known everything—"

"—everything about you—"

"—when you had never met before—"

"—yes, how?"

Samuel opened his eyes which immediately found and focused on the mauve woolen flower just beyond his nose. With much effort he lifted his hand and traced a finger around the rose's perimeter, then curled his palm around one side as if cupping it, protecting it from our vision. His eyes brimmed with tears. His lovely lower lip, soft and red as a ripening plum, began to quiver. And he sobbed, "I . . . she . . . the shape of my soul . . . knew it . . . she and still . . . oh, God . . . still *smiled!*"

His eyes closed and his sobbing began to fade away. Our own eyes were quite wide, our mouths agape (one of us seemed to be panting) as we waited for him to bring the story to a suitable conclusion. But he did not move. His breathing became shallow. We lifted his eyelids—so thin, so translucent as if made of the finest porcelain—and saw only the whites of his eyes. We prodded him, gently slapped him, removed some jonquils from a vase and poured the water over him.

He gasped like a newborn taking its first breath and cried out, "Fishing!"

We held his face between our palms, gently shaking it, and said, "Yes, yes, yes, fishing. Go on."

And he said, "Earthworms!"

"Yes, yes, go *on!*"

He looked at us sleepily, his eyes rolling from side to side, from top to bottom. "How could she have known?" he wondered aloud.

"Yes, how, Samuel?" we wondered aloud too, though the small section of our brain that was still sober also wondered (secretly, of course) why we wished to know this particular answer rather than, say, the answer to: *What does her father do for a living?*

We saw that he was fading again and so pinched his nose and slapped him (a bit harder this time, leaving a five-fingered crimson imprint across his feverish cheeks). When he spoke, his voice was barely audible thus we were forced to press our ears against his lips in order to hear him say, with disappointing finality: "Her brown fingers . . . the pink worms . . . curled . . . so pretty . . . so extraordinarily . . . terribly . . . *oh God in Heaven!* . . . pretty."

We did not speak of that evening again—not among ourselves, and certainly not to Samuel's father or mother, neither of whom had been present that evening, though it was their house and their wine (as well as their son) with which we had taken liberties. Samuel's parents who, thank god, were vacationing in Greece at the time, growing tan on beaches or yachts, refreshing their classical history and Greek mythology, never once suspecting (who would suspect?) that friends they had known over half their lives were, on another continent, undressing their drunken semiconscious son, putting him to bed (all the while politely ignoring his rather bold erection), making certain to turn him on his left side toward the brass wastecan, to draw the blinds and the curtains, to place two aspirin and a glass of water on his nightstand, to wipe away the spittle that was gathering at the side of his mouth, and finally to lock the front door behind us as we departed quietly, warily, as if leaving the scene of an unconscionable crime.

It was a crime. We knew it. Thus we did not speak of it again. (Although for a month or so afterward, each time we ordered wine with dinner, we blushed.)

Samuel—dear to our hearts! precious to our souls!—remembered nothing. Certainly not enough to indict us. Occasionally, however, when teasing him about his affaire de coeur, begging him for descriptions of the girl, details of her genealogy, her education, her bank account, and, so as not to arouse suspicion of their first meeting—Samuel would throw out tiny scraps of information, all the while staring pensively at the back of his hands, and conclude with, "I've said this before, haven't I? I'm quite certain I've told you this before."

To which we would respond, laughing gaily, "No, no, of course not! You must be thinking of someone else. Someone else *entirely.*" And we, cleverly adding: "Besides, dear, we wouldn't need to ask at all if you would just bring the girl along with you next time you visit. Bring her to dinner, please?"

Until finally he did.

Therefore, that evening in autumn:

The sun shining on the rear westward side of Evelyn's house. The front and eastern side in shadow. And Samuel and Claudia standing on the portico, within the shadow, huddled against one another and shivering almost imperceptibly, as if cold—though the air was still quite warm from the midday heat.

Claudia was not the beauty we had imagined. She was in fact rather plain, save for her long black hair shining blue and her black eyes which seemed to recede into infinity, into the most distant past—that split second before the creation of the world, perhaps (we now hypothesize) more distant than even that. She wore an inappropriate mohair sweater (obviously hand-knitted and much too large for her small frame) over a simple white blouse and beige skirt that hung (unfashionably) a half-inch above her rather knotty kneecaps.

Samuel, of course, was as dapper as ever except for one glaring flaw: A dandelion, wilted and turning brown at the edges, protruded from the breast pocket of his blazer, just below the starched white handkerchief that was now soiled by the decaying yellow-brown weed. We stared at it, suppressing (with painful effort) the urge to pluck the hideous thing from his pocket and make him perfect, while he grinned at us and placed his hand against the small of Claudia's back and pushed her forward into the foyer, brushing his lips against the back of her head, against her black hair, briefly closing his eyes and inhaling.

Introductions were made all around, and as each of us reached for Claudia's thin brown hand we could not help but imagine a long pink earthworm wriggling upon her tapered fingers. Then when we actually grasped the hand and found it in fact cold and damp, we shuddered, battling the small waves of nausea rising in our throats—which made it ever so difficult to welcome her in the elegantly hospitable way to which we (if not the girl herself) were accustomed.

We stepped away from the young couple, making a straight path for them into the dining hall, allowing them to enter first, watching them for a moment before following after them. Noticing the way they leaned into one another, whispering, it seemed, without opening their mouths. Noticing Samuel's large hand partially lost beneath Claudia's long hair which trailed behind her like a veil of black satin. Noticing her index finger and thumb pinching the hem of his blazer—her tenuous solitary hold on him. Noticing, finally, that the shoes on her feet were not shoes at all but sandals—raw-looking, probably from Peru or Bolivia, perhaps from her mother's poor mountain village, hand-hewn by an old Indian with unsteady fingers and failing vision.

At this last revelation, we frowned to ourselves in such a way that each of us (utterly in agreement) knew we were frowning to ourselves.

And then Evelyn's dinner with her bad baby carrots.

And then the leaping and dying sparks.

And then our old friend Chas and his solitary (senile?) remark on the world.

And then Claudia's confident response: "No. It is a perfect world. And I have seen its perfection."

And what of youth?

What of the moment just before youth becomes . . . becomes *what?* Non-youth? Or are we correct in referring to it as adulthood? Labels, we have come to believe (believe in private, of course), are much less important than the contents therein. For example: if a label says "Poison" and you wish to die—die before the unbearable pain of age sets in—and so drink of the labeled contents and consequently find yourself living—terribly sick perhaps, but regrettably alive—then what good was the label? What practical use did it supply?

Consider now our loss: Not only of youth, but of belief. The belief, as it were, in everything—love, magic, God, perfection. . . . Belief like a chrysalis, transparent and thin to the imago, something to leave behind. But to the caterpillar? Nothing but the irrefutable shape of the universe, inside of which miracles perpetually occur.

We are, however, neither caterpillar nor butterfly, forced through metamorphosis by the unyielding hand of God. Certainly our bodies age, dry out, grow weak, fall apart, eventually die. But our souls are not governed by time or space or the cruel whims of nature—are they? Cannot youth, for the soul, be an endless thing—spawning therefore endless belief and thus: infinite love and magic and God and perfection . . . ?

We ask these questions silently as we lie in our beds at night, sleeplessly shifting from one tired bone to another. Wanting (but afraid) to weep at the memory of what we have lost. Recalling with an aching melancholia Claudia's black eyes which, from beyond infinity, doubted absolutely nothing, believed in everything. And Samuel: His eyes so full of love for Claudia that he had no choice but to also believe.

Perhaps if we had known the girl, known at least her socio-economic background, we would have also known how we should respond to her somewhat shocking premise: "No. It is a perfect world. And I have seen its perfection."

But Samuel had left us so poorly informed that when we thought of her at all, we thought first and foremost of *earthworms*, for heaven's sake! Furthermore, our own speculations were simply that: speculations. We did not want to risk being wrong, nor risk the possibility (slim as it was) that she might very well be the niece of Dr Eduardo Martinez or some other upstanding, financially powerful and highly influential member of our community. (We did not, after all, even know the girl's last name!) As it were, we simply smiled at her, then at Samuel who did not see our smiles meant for him because his vision was full of only Claudia, his ears tuned only toward her voice.

Ignored thusly by Samuel, we turned our smiles once again on Claudia who glanced away from us and down at her brandy.

"I see that you don't believe me," she said quietly, amusement flickering at the corners of her mouth.

And before we could deny the accusation Samuel denied it for us, reaching a hand out to touch Claudia's fingers curled around her snifter, stating matter-of-factly, "Of course they believe you, sweetie." Then he turned to us with such an eager and gently threatening expression, adding, *"Don't you?"* that we had no other option but to nod stupidly and mumble our apologetic confirmations.

Claudia looked up from her snifter and softly chuckled—a chuckle which Samuel evidently misconstrued as one of mild chagrin, for he chuckled too and said, "That's right, sweetie, that's right. They *do* believe you."

However, we did not. Nor did we misconstrue: It was not chagrin that made the chuckle rise in Claudia's throat. No, she was laughing at us. We knew it. She, laughing that sort of world-weary pitying laugh which we'd heard often enough before from dying intellectuals, apathetic liberals, and famous-but-impoverished socialists. The difference being that Claudia was at least thirty years younger than these others—too young, we thought, to be weary of anything, least of all the world. And certainly too poorly attired to be pitying *us* (not a single one of whom was dressed in anything less than imported silk or gabardine).

And perhaps it was this one discrepancy—a discrepancy in age and thus legitimate rights to weariness and/or pity—which caused our old friend Chas to suddenly seat himself in a stiff armchair, cross his legs, clear his throat and loudly state, "I don't believe you, young lady, but I would be more than happy to hear your testimony."

To which Samuel curtly replied, "No."

To which Claudia gently contradicted, "Yes."

To which we silently exulted: *A lover's quarrel!*

But, alas, that was the end of it: Claudia won.

The sun had dropped just below the treeline, thus the sky was still lit with a pale, watery grayness and there were no shadows on the lawn. The wind had increased so much in strength that it had begun howling, screeching, tearing the leaves from their branches and bending the great geyser of Evelyn's fountain into a shuddering arc which hissed across the terrace. The occasional brave, mindless bird who attempted to perch on the white marble scallop of the fountain's rim was immediately blown off into the spray and consequently did not hesitate long before taking shelter in a nook of the nearest tree.

Samuel moved behind Claudia, sadly touching (or more precisely cupping) her shoulder, rolling it once beneath his palm. He closed the French doors but the wind's howling remained. A howling we found terribly unsettling—the fierceness of it, that is, the anger—as if it foretold (cruelly) the cold and bitter winter that was to come. Or worse: foretold our impending deaths and the judgments which would follow—though we did not necessarily believe in an afterlife or certainly did not consider the possibility often, not even those of us who attended church with some frequency—attending more out of habit, of course, than desire. An afterlife in which we did not necessarily believe because, well, its existence had never been proved. (Later—alone, of course, and silently—we would consider the implications of believing only in what is proved. In other words, having no belief at all since what is proved is *known,* not believed.) That evening, amid the unsettling howl of the wind, we did not afford ourselves the leisure of semantics.

Claudia seated herself on a petit point footstool near Samuel's feet—Samuel who, staring tragically down upon the blue-black oval of the girl's head, was so overcome with emotion *(love,* we can only imagine) that he found it necessary to back away from her, taking two slow measured steps and then bumping into the wall toward which he then turned and stared in surprise, as if it were an old friend or enemy who had suddenly leaped out of his past and into his immediate future. To complete the analogy, Samuel nodded at the wall and turned away from it, blushing and befuddled—turned to look at us who looked back at him, smiling tiny smiles of endearment and, yes, our own brand of pity. Pity for a young man so much in love that social graces have gone wholly awry, have become useless words to carelessly toss at walls, for heaven's sake, rather than tactical weapons to aim at people. *Pity:* For we had been there ourselves once upon a time. Blindly, hopelessly—ah, yes!—*desperately* in love. And we did not want to go back, or if we did would not confess to such a puerile desire since we were, at our age and in our social circle, expected to have outgrown such crass passions. Thus, we smiled our tiny, endearing, pitying smiles, thinking: *Poor, poor, effusive Samuel!*

Then Claudia began to speak and, for the time being, we forgot all about him.

"I used to despise the world," she said, her voice one octave higher than the wind's. "I considered it a generally awful place. Evil, evil. A morass of petty wars, needless hunger . . . a hundred different faces of cruelty and deceit." She looked at each of us in turn, and then looked down into her brandy, smiling faintly (as always) and studying the golden liquid (of which she had not tasted a single drop, just as she had—rudely, we thought—rejected the pre-duck chardonnay and the with-duck merlot and the post-duck sauterne)—studying the brandy as if it contained some magnificent vision into which she could peer and see, well . . . *everything*.

(Note here that we were already beginning to dislike that little smile of hers, believing it to be a judgment against us and not "a manifestation of perfect spiritual serenity," as Samuel later claimed, a claim over which we now occasionally mull—mulling, of course, solitarily at night as we reach our mottled fingers toward elusive sleep, reaching warily, always suspecting it shall be our final sleep, a sleep with no waking—no waking at least into *this* life, *this* world—and more frightened perhaps of that place into which we, having died, shall wake eternally.)

We stood our ground against Claudia's smile, biting our tongues, displaying the tolerance borne out of wisdom and years and good breeding—all of us except Chas who every now and then mumbled a "hmph" or "tss" and brusquely tapped his cigar against the rim of his snifter, the ashes quietly dropping into the half-inch of brandy below. And his thin (oh, lately how thin!) legs jerking and twitching with undisguised irritation.

Then she, Claudia, suddenly turned and smiled at Samuel who squatted morosely with his back pressed flat against the very same wall to which he had earlier apologized. He stared back at her, unsmiling, obviously pained, and slowly mouthed the words: "Please, don't."

If Claudia gave a response we did not hear it. Instead we watched her hold her brandy snifter toward him, which he took obediently, squatting now with two full drinks in his hands, blind and idiotic in love.

"And because I despised the world," continued Claudia, suddenly turning toward us, "I tried to escape it." At which point she pushed up her mohair sleeves, unbuttoned the cuffs of her blouse and held up her hands, exhibiting with neither shame nor pride the pinkish purple scars streaking down her wrists.

We gasped, "Oh, my!"

Chas muttered, "Ah-*ha!*"

Samuel closed his eyes, out of which dribbled two tears—one from his left eye and one from his right—making their way downward toward the tip of his aristocratic nose from which they dropped, one at a time, into Claudia's untasted brandy.

"And I succeeded," Claudia said, smiling (always smiling). "I died."

Ah, and then death: *The final acquisition,* as George (Evelyn's late) used to say, before he himself succumbed to that last inevitable purchase.

We saw him die, watched him accomplish the feat in a matter of minutes: his square body (broad-chested and short and slightly fat over the hardened muscles) clothed in white cotton, marching toward us across the terrace of the clubhouse, a tennis racket swinging at his side, gripped in his right fist like a rifle, the red blotchy flesh of his face shining with sweat and victory; and he, dropping himself into a chair beneath our umbrella, snatching up a croissant with his left hand and taking a large, rather gluttonous bite and then, quite immediately, before swallowing even, squeezing the croissant into a ball of dough, staring in wide-eyed bewilderment at the bundled fist, and then at us, his mouth opening and closing like a fish out of water, his tongue slowly spilling out between his lips, topped with the sodden mound of half-chewed bread, a sort of dry gurgling from his throat, a wet gurgling from his posterior, then the clatter of his tennis racket as it fell onto the hot red bricks of the terrace. And we, leaning toward him like tall blades of grass pulled forward by the wind of a passing automobile, struck mute, horrified and simultaneously awed by the immeasurable strength of death, able to defeat George Wilton in a matter of not more than two hundred seconds. George Wilton: who was only fifty-seven. Who, according to our recollections, had not lost a tennis match in over twenty years.

Thus we are familiar with the unbecoming face of death. And in our familiarity often pray to God (though we do not necessarily *believe* in God, considering the lack of substantial evidence)—we pray that if we must die then let it be at night, when we are alone and silent and reaching toward sleep: *Let us die in our sleep, God. And for godsake, God, do not let us die with our tongues hanging out of our mouths.*

Claudia, looking very much alive, carefully buttoned up her sleeves (the cuffs of which, we could not help but notice, were discolored and worn), saying, "But let me digress . . ." And then she pulled down her mohair sleeves, smoothed them out, and laid her hands in the beige sinkhole of her lap.

"It was the morning of my twenty-fifth birthday. I was awakened by the sound of a thief breaking my bedroom window. I lived in an old brownstone, on the fifth floor. The thief, the *boy*—he couldn't have been more than fourteen—had climbed up the fire escape in broad daylight, wearing a red jacket and baseball cap, and a jimmy hooked through a belt loop of his jeans. Pretty brazen, don't you think—a red jacket, a jimmy in plain view, the sound of breaking glass at seven o'clock in the morning? Of course he knew that no one gave a damn. If any one of my neighbors leaped out of bed and ran to their windows that morning, I'm sure they just as quickly went back to bed once they figured out it wasn't their apartment being burglarized. There were at least a hundred other apartments on that street. Forty in my building alone. Yet he chose mine. On the fifth floor! How *wonderful!*"

And she laughed.

And we considered then, for the first time that day, how nearly pretty Claudia was when she laughed: her coppery lips pulled back over straight white teeth, her black eyes twinkling from within that deep, distant, private infinity of hers. And seeing her thusly, we understood (with a sudden and astounding clarity) the poignant moment on the museum's wet lawn four months previous, when she had looked up at Samuel, already smiling, and he had sensed that she knew everything about him. For we sensed it too, there in Evelyn's living room, in front of the waning fire— and it was not (we admit) an unpleasant sensation at all. In fact, it made our bodies feel less constricting, our mottled skin and squeaking joints inconsequential, our graying hair resembling (as Samuel might have put it) *glorious fibers of pure and dazzling ethereal light.*

It's true: Claudia's smile made us feel, briefly, quite thoroughly, *free.*

(We took quick sips of brandy in order to stifle our sudden giddiness.)

"So," said Claudia, "I awoke to shattering glass and a boy, a *child,* standing in a glittering rectangle of sunlight and shards, momentarily blinded by the darkness beyond, squinting and blinking beneath the bill of his red cap, looking around the room, looking right at me but not seeing me for a long time. Until I asked, *Are you going to kill me?* And he jumped and gave a little cry—a high-pitched, squeaking exclamation like a frightened rabbit—and then pulled his jimmy from his belt loop and held it in front of him, toward me, like a crucifix.

"I repeated the question, more slowly this time: *Are you going to kill me?*

"And he stammered: *N-n-not if you don't scream or n-n-nothin'.*

"And I said: *Then I will scream.* And I filled my lungs with air.

"He shook the jimmy/crucifix at me and cried: *No no please lady, don't scream, don't scream!*

"And I said: *Why not? You promised to kill me if I screamed. Are you now saying that you intend to welsh on your promise? That you won't kill me, after all?*

"He stared at me a while, then lowered the jimmy to his side and dropped his shoulders and let his head roll backward and closed his eyes and said out loud, *Oh, man, I had to get a crazy one, didn't I? And* he looked at me. *You a crazy one, ain't you, huh?*

"I yawned, rubbed the sleep from my eyes, propped my elbow on my knee, my chin on my hand, and told him: *No, I'm not crazy. I'm just awfully tired. Awfully disgusted.*

"He gave me a blank look, so I added: *I hate the world.*

"And he said: *Yeah, me too, lady, but I don't go aroun' askin' no strangers to beat me over the head with no crowbar.*

"*A jimmy,* I told him.

"He said, *Huh?*

"I said, *That's a jimmy you're holding, not a crowbar. A jimmy is exactly like a crowbar except it's smaller. I'm sure it has some legitimate uses, but I think it's primarily used by burglars to break into houses and apartments.*

"He looked at the jimmy in his hand and then back at me and smiled. *So I'm usin' it the right way, huh?*

"I nodded at him. *Some people also use it as a weapon,* I added, pointing to my head and winking.

"He gave me a look of disgust and fear and then laid the jimmy on my bureau alongside a couple of perfume bottles and a hairbrush. *I ain't gonna do that,* he told me, crossing his skinny arms over his chest. *I seen too many dead people to wanna make more of 'em. And I tell you what. I seen a person die slow and I seen a baby born quick, and the bornin' was better. It was beautiful, man. Man, it was really beautiful. So, see, I got my rules. Maybe you got yours, too, but they your rules and not mine, see?*

"*Unfortunately,* I told him, *you're standing in my apartment. Mine.*

"*Wha——?* he asked. I repeated myself. He looked down at his feet, around the room once, then back at me and said, *But I'm stealing here, lady, it ain't the same thing.*

"*Fine,* I said, grabbing my bathrobe. I threw it on over my T-shirt and moved toward the bathroom. *You steal, then. You take everything I own. As you can see there isn't a helluva lot, but whatever you think you can sell on the street, you take it. It's yours, babe. I don't want it anymore.* And then I walked into the bathroom, closed the door and cut my wrists wide open."

Thus far, we had listened attentively, motionless—except Chas who, his thin legs twitching and bouncing, punctuated Claudia's story with an occasional snort or incoherent mumble. But now we could not help but lean toward her, just a bit, stopping ourselves short before we reached our hands out to catch her in our imaginations, catch her as we envisioned her falling then: flesh opened like the tight, soft skin of fruit, her young thick blood pulsing from the wounds, flooding the floor, soaking her bathrobe, her T-shirt, matting her black hair, spurting into her black eyes where the depth was slowly fading away, obscured by the premature glaze of death.

Samuel inhaled loudly, slowly, pathetically. And when he exhaled, the words that slid out on that similarly pathetic breath were so full of childlike grief that we forgot, for a moment, Claudia's slit wrists and concentrated our hearts on Samuel— dear, beloved Samuel! So much like our own son! Stirring awake our paternalistic and/or maternalistic natures. Samuel, who had (while our attention was turned elsewhere) drunk the contents of both snifters in his hands and was now vaguely intoxicated.

"Don't go on," he told her, pathetically.

Claudia looked down at her hands.

"*Please,*" begged Samuel. Then to us: "Don't let her go on. This is *mine.* Don't take it away. This one thing . . . *please* . . . let me have for my own?"

We stared at him, momentarily confused. (Chas theatrically laid the side of his head against his palm and loudly yawned, and for the briefest moment we hated our old friend Chas.) And then we understood:

Samuel had heard the story before. All of it. From beginning to end. Perhaps drawing it from Claudia one morning after having made love to her, after having kissed the faintly callused palms of her brown hands only to discover the hideous scars below them. And he, mute, stammering for a moment over the pinkish purple ridges, then blurting out: *"When? Oh, sweetie, why?"* We understood: Samuel (by now having heard the story how many times?) had come to view the tale as a gruesome symbol of an inviolate union, a hideous, sacred thing. Hideous but *shared*. Ah, yes! Samuel the poet! Samuel the romantic— *hopeless!* Mistaking the girl's early act of confidence as a most indisputable gesture of love and faith and trust. And when had he ever known such things? When had *anyone* shared with him a secret wish, a hidden hope, an unspeakable dread? Certainly not his father (too shrewd) nor his mother (too . . . well, we weren't quite certain *what*). And certainly not us. We did not share. It wasn't in our nature to share (or if it was, we had quickly learned to suppress it, knowing that when you share a secret with another you may as well hand them a loaded gun, saying, "Pull the trigger, please!").

And so perhaps that stricken look on Samuel's face—the one that caused our paternalistic and/or maternalistic love to swell inside of us—was the result of his losing a first and certainly very large secret. (Unable to *own* yet another thing of love in a long line of perhaps lovable but highly useless things: dogs without breeding, newspaper kites, dime store pocket knives, friends with bad grammar, old cars with big tires, girls with red-painted lips, summer in Zaire, poetry . . .) Losing it to us, no less. Whereupon it would henceforward be classified as public knowledge. Nothing more, nothing less, and certainly not a secret.

We did not respond to Samuel's request, pretended deafness, for we did in fact want the girl's story, her secret infinite knowledge. And now, after Samuel's pleading, we wanted it more than ever. You see, at that point in our lives and economies there was so very little left in the world which we could *not* have—except youth, of course. Youth and its charming accoutrements of love, magic, God, perfection. . . . Youth and Claudia's secret. Which we secretly hoped (hoped with a fluttering of hearts—our tired, aging hearts with their blocked arteries, leaking valves, late-night palpitations, and early-morning angina pectoris)—hoped would give us back our youth, our belief, and consequently: love, magic, God, perfection. . . . Give us back not only the courage to live, but also the courage to die.

Claudia smiled at Samuel without turning around—a sweet affectionate smile, like a mother's for her child—and reached her hand out behind her like a blind girl, reached for him and, finding his knee, pressed her fingers tightly against it and then withdrew them: a gesture which shifted Samuel's pleading attention from us and made him glance down in time to see Claudia's hand moving away from his knee, his cheeks subsequently rising with color, not (we assumed) from embarrassment but from an involuntary burst of sexual excitement which caused him to finally lose his balance and fall, gracefully, to the floor. Where he would remain, silently resigned, for the duration of Claudia's story.

"There was nothing unusual," said Claudia, "about my apartment building. It was a typical old brownstone, built in the fifties and since then maintained with tight-assed economy—a little paint every year, a new lock on the door, perhaps a new piece of plumbing here and there as the old rusted out. The bathroom floor was tiled with those small white octagons that were, when you laid your head down on them, icy cold regardless of the temperature inside or out. After I'd lost a great deal of blood, after I'd grown so weak that I could no longer hold my head up, I laid it down on the little white tiles and their coldness shocked me. I opened my eyes and looked out at them and saw . . . a pattern of discoloration . . . a deep yellowing near the molding, growing cleaner and whiter as it moved away from the wall, toward the spot where I lay. And in that split second—a moment simultaneously brief and infinite— in that moment I recognized the simple, ordinary, and yet *absolutely perfect* . . . The pattern of discoloration was flawless, you see. *Flawless.* No human being could have duplicated . . . And all of it just an accumulation of dirt and time. There . . . I saw . . . with some glorious inner eye of the soul . . . saw with startling perspicacity, as if blinders had been lifted from . . . not my eyes . . . no, not . . . I *saw* in the most abstract sense of the word, I saw . . . "

She paused breathlessly.

"For godsake, saw *what?*" we shouted, wide-eyed, our feet automatically sliding toward her, our heads automatically stretching forward, pulling the sagging skin of our necks taut.

Claudia smiled and shook her head in pity. "Oh, how can I explain it to you?"

"Try!" we demanded.

She spread her arms wide and tilted her head toward the ceiling and said slowly, loudly, just as the wind outside let loose a terrifying long shrill howl: "I saw the world in its entirety. Its beginning and its end. Saw its wars, kindness, hunger, laughter, poverty, lust, love . . . saw *everything* . . . all at once . . . in perfect harmony. As if I had, for an instant, seen through an angel's eyes. Or more precisely, seen with—God forgive me, what a *sacrilege* this must seem!—seen with the *omnipotent eye of God!*"

We did not gasp. We did not breathe.

Claudia slowly lowered her arms and laughed. "I can't begin to describe the joy I felt. It was boundless, infinite. It lifted me up—literally. I raised myself up from the cold tiles and, desperately trying to hold onto everything I'd witnessed, trying to formulate it all into words . . . an effort which was, of course, futile —there is no language capable of explaining knowledge so pure and complete. I crawled to the bathroom door and reached for the knob and slowly turned it and shouted, I thought, thought

I shouted, though in reality my voice couldn't have been more than a whisper—shouted through the crack in the door at the boy-thief sifting through my bureau—shouted, *I understand everything, my God, I understand!* And the boy must have heard me, or perhaps seen in the reflection of the mirror before him, seen a growing pool of blood spilling into the rectangle of sunlight on the floor, since he suddenly spun around and threw himself backward against the edge of the bureau and gave a scream, horrified, screamed out: *Oh Jesus oh Jesus oh God have mercy!* And then dropped the pile of socks in his hand and ran to me, pushing open the bathroom door, grabbing towels and tying them tightly below my elbows, all the while crying, *"Don't you die, lady! Shit man oh shit don't you die!* And what I remember last is looking up into the boy's frightened face streaked with tears and sweat . . . looking up and smiling at him from what seemed to be such a great distance . . . a steadily growing distance . . . looking up and smiling and saying over and over and over again, *It's perfect, you know, perfect . . . perfect . . ."*

The sun had vanished altogether, taking with it the last residue of light. The wind had never relented: Though it no longer shrieked its wounded-banshee shriek, no longer howled, its low insistent moaning seemed to envelope Evelyn's house, pushing against doors and windows, against the stone walls, making the air within the room seem a bit too thin, too warm, bad. Bad air. The fire was nearly out—not even a hiss from it— and the red embers were the only source of light in the room.

We wondered: How long had we stood there, in the darkness, listening to Claudia's story? And how could it have been darkness since we remembered looking into her face as she spoke, remembered her black eyes and thin mouth with its flickering, pitying smile, the tilting of her head to one side or the other, bending on her long neck so much like a dark swan's? And when, we asked ourselves, had Samuel moved away from the wall to plant himself at Claudia's side, where he now bent his head low, gathering up her hands which lay like sleeping doves in her lap, and lifting them to his face, to his lips, kissing them hard to stop his mouth from quivering, the tears washing down his face unhindered but silent? And Chas—when had he stopped his grating interjections, stopped twitching, and dunked the tip of his cigar into his brandy and fallen to sleep—awkwardly, his head tilted sharply to one side, his mouth agape.

Although Claudia offered a polite pause—allowing us, no doubt, a chance to question, declaim, challenge—we found ourselves at a loss for words, a position we had not experienced since . . . well, we could not remember when. Furthermore, our brandies were empty (though we did not recall having taken the last sip) and we therefore could not deflect attention from our speechlessness by putting a snifter to our lips.

Fortunately, Evelyn (playing the role of houseboy with a sense of pride that verged on outright arrogance) chose that moment to rekindle the dying fire, grunting and groaning as she hefted an oversized log onto the andirons, creating a visual explosion as it tumbled onto the embers, after which she stood up, brushed her hands clean, propped them on her hips and smiled (proudly, arrogantly) at the rest of us who would have been more than willing to smile back at her if our snifters had not been empty.

Claudia put her arm around Samuel's broad, trembling shoulders and kissed his auburn hair. And though she still smiled that odd faint smile of hers, we could see now, in the rising light of the fireplace, that she also wept: her small tears tangling in her lashes, never making it any farther than the slight hollow beneath her eyes. And yet her voice was steady and certain of itself when she hurried forward toward the end of her defense.

"I don't know what happened to the boy, the thief. I do know that it was him who called the ambulance, it must have been him. They came quickly—not soon enough to stop me from dying, but soon enough to resuscitate me. And I could tell you about life after death, too—tell you about a tiny fragment of it, the beginning of eternity—but that is another story and one you maybe should discover for yourselves."

She glanced over her shoulder at the night which stood like an impatient and unwanted visitor outside the French doors, and once again bent down to kiss Samuel's head. "It's time to go," she told him quietly.

We suddenly sprang to life, waving our hands through the air, throwing them to our hearts, saying, "No, no—"

"—don't leave yet—"

"—please—"

"—stay a while longer—"

"—oh, yes, stay—"

"—the night—"

"—is but a pup!"

But Samuel lifted himself from Claudia's lap, and Claudia rose from the petit point and said, "Thank you, but our plane leaves awfully early tomorrow morning."

To which we exclaimed in unison: "What plane?"

Samuel took Claudia's right hand with his left, thrust his other into a pocket of his trousers and nonchalantly studied the ceiling, then his shoes.

"You didn't tell them," Claudia said, her disappointment restrained but discernible.

"No," said Samuel. "I thought it best . . . " He looked at us apologetically. "I thought it best to inform all of you later."

"Inform us of what?" we asked nervously.

He looked at Claudia, who looked back at him, smiling faintly but hesitantly as he pulled his shoulders straight, looked at us squarely, and stated with an onrush of words which followed so closely together that they nearly overlapped: "We're to be married Claudia and I and we shall go to live in the mountains in the Andes and have many children and teach them to love the world and love what is hideous as well as what is beautiful love poetry and silence flowers and weeds storms and tranquillity life and death love it all as a single thing which in fact it is a single thing and perfect just as Claudia says absolutely undeniably perfect this world."

To which Claudia supported with a clear and melodious, "Yes."

To which we responded, "No."

Samuel's face fell. Claudia's hardened.

"You will not leave us," we told Samuel, forcing a rigidness into our voices which we had not, as we recalled, used in many years, not since our own children had attempted a (losing) battle for their independence.

"I will," said Samuel, and then pulling Claudia to him, added, "*We* will."

Well, of course we didn't care one way or another whether Claudia stayed or went—never mind her brief glance into infinite wisdom and death. We did not know her and furthermore suspected she was not of our *ilk,* so to speak. It was Samuel we wanted with us. Dear Samuel, *our* Samuel—young, handsome, rich! So much more a son to us than our own sons, more a part of us than our right arms—arms which lately did not function precisely as we wished them to, sometimes causing us embarrassment and great pain—pain not as severe, however, as that which Samuel now was inflicting without mercy upon us. And in order to stop the pain we found it necessary to resort to weaponry we had not used since . . . well, since Samuel had wished to become a poet, for heaven's sake.

We aimed. We fired: "Does your father know of your plans?"

Samuel's pale skin went paler, then flushed. He stammered: "No, I . . . I . . . I . . ."

Claudia said, "We have every intention of telling him. And Samuel's mother, too. After we've reached our destination."

"I see," we said. "And your plane leaves tomorrow morning?"

They nodded.

We looked at each other, void of expression, but void in such a way that each of us knew what the other was feeling and thinking and plotting—each of us except Chas, who was still asleep, lightly snoring, a long string of saliva stretching from the corner of his mouth down to his lovely blue necktie, his snifter tipped to one side and spilling, with each respiration, a globule of black brandy-sodden ashes onto the crotch of his trousers. We shuddered and looked away.

Moving toward the young couple huddled there by the French doors against which the wind mercilessly pummeled itself, we offered our hands, saying, "Well, good luck then—"

"—best of luck—"

" —to you both—"

" —terribly good to meet you, Claudia—"

"—yes, terribly—"

"—Samuel, you'll write, of course—"

"—oh, yes, write—"

"—won't you?"

And Samuel grinned and let his shoulders relax and shook our hands and kissed our cheeks, and there were hugs all around and many kisses and a fluttering of hands like torn flags waving at the young couple as they trotted down the front steps of Evelyn's house, the cruel wind miraculously avoiding them, skirting around them, moaning its gloomy judgment from a seemingly far distance, as they, Samuel and Claudia, stepped into the darkness and out of sight.

O God, forgive our loneliness!

This, a little prayer-of-sorts that pops into our heads every now and then.

During the day, the demands of business or shopping suffice to distract us. But at night, ah! At night loneliness comes slinking into the room, crouched low, waiting. Waiting until the book we are reading or the brief we are preparing or the television program we are watching no longer holds our interest and so we put it aside. Loneliness inevitably preceded by boredom—the boredom settling around us like a sleepy cat, then the loneliness pouncing, bearing the whole of its weight down upon our chests until we believe our ribs will shatter and all the air, all the *life,* will whistle out of us as if we were nothing more than a solitary balloon, punctured by the pointedness of our own solitude.

Thus: We acquire, seize, cling. And occasionally sputter an accidental prayer.

Each year the winters grow longer. So much longer that it often seems we shall perish before the arrival of spring. Thus we are profoundly grateful when it finally arrives.

And perhaps it was, therefore, out of such gratitude that Evelyn proposed an alfresco brunch *(shish kebabs,* for heaven's sake!) and what's more, croquet—wishing, she explained, to re-create an old-fashioned, all-American (meaning *middle-class)* Saturday "get-together," although we secretly suspected the shish kebabs were the consequence of Evelyn's habitual flipping through women's magazines at the supermarket (she still does her own shopping, too), and the croquet a noble attempt to keep everyone off the tennis courts which she believes (not surprisingly—*poor deceased George!)* to be fatal.

So there we were, dressed all in white, hunched over the wickets, plotting and scheming against one another (all in fun, of course), dodging the gray billows of smoke rolling from the barbecue pit over the verdant lawn, and trying our damnedest to bite our tongues as Samuel poured himself *yet another* Bloody Mary (though it was not even ten o'clock in the morning), pouring his fifth, we were certain (we were counting), and carelessly spilling it on the cuffs of his white silk shirt, not even bothering to wipe at it with the linen napkin handed to him by Evelyn as she hurried past on her way to the barbecue pit, which now seemed to be on fire.

Yes: We bit our tongues and watched, peripherally, as he tipped his head back and poured a half-glass of tomato juice and vodka down his throat, swaying from side to side as he swallowed, then lowered the glass and squinted up at the sun, wiping his brow with his cuff and thus smearing it with the tomato juice. We, watching—even as we took aim against our opponents—watching lest he fall onto the red bricks of Evelyn's terrace and bruise himself (his skin so pale, you see, so delicate) —all of us watching, except Chas who instead watched the shish kebabs, now aflame, watched with a deep and violent scowl of irritation etched into his forehead (his sad, angry forehead, freckled with age and as dry now as an old handbag).

But Samuel did not fall, at least not onto the bricks. Instead he sort of crumpled: bent precisely in half and dropped, posterior first, into the nearest chaise. He lay there a moment, baffled by something we could not see but which evidently stood precisely among us, for that is where he stared, wide-eyed, his handsome face hideously distorted by the bewildering thing which he viewed with horror. And we, growing uncomfortable (perhaps even afraid) at the thought of something so ... so *foreign* in our midst, concerned that it might at any given moment reach out its thin, cold, damp fingers and grab hold, pull us into its own world of what: poverty, war, hunger, disease?

(We shuddered to think of it.)

And then Samuel suddenly withdrew his stare, looked up at the blue sky, then quickly down at the red bricks of the terrace, pointed, and cried out, "Look!"

We dropped our mallets on the lawn and ran toward him and huddled around the spot at which he aimed his finger.

"An earthworm," he said.

We stooped a bit and peered at the bricks. It was indeed an earthworm: pink and wet and writhing on the hot, red surface.

"It fell from the sky," said Samuel.

We looked up, simultaneously ducking our heads, expecting more of the same.

Samuel, of course, believed the worm to be a sign, a message of love and forgiveness from Claudia—mythical, magical, *believing* Claudia, an ephemeral angel resurrected from death. She

would never, we realized, exist as anything less to him. Therefore: although Samuel physically had remained with us (what
choice did his father give him but to remain?), a very large part
of him—youthful, credulous, spiritual—had departed with the
girl and was now living alongside her in some remote mountain village in Bolivia or Peru (we can't remember which),
where she was, is, and no doubt shall forever be, contemplating
the perfection of the world.

Yet we who had already lived so long without youth and
belief, we knew it was an ordinary bird that had dropped the
worm. A robin, most likely, on its way to feed its young—flying
over the Wilton estate and then singing out some unnecessary
warning or lament, stupidly opening its beak and consequently
dropping the worm onto Evelyn's terrace.

An ordinary bird! Though we did not state this aloud. Instead
we looked down at the wriggling creature losing moisture on
the hot, red bricks, drying up, *dying,* although it was no more
than three inches from the safe, wet world of grass.

"Fishing," said Samuel, his face now drawn in unspeakable
sadness, a tear plummeting down his flushed cheek.

To which we replied, "Yes?"

To which he responded, "That first day . . . we went fishing,
Claudia and I. We took the jar of earthworms to the lake and
rented a canoe and paddled out to the middle and . . ." He
paused, took a gulp of his Bloody Mary (a portion of which slid
down his chin and landed in a startling puddle of red against his
white silk tie), then he looked up at us, looked at each of us, one
by one, and said, "I placed a worm on the hook myself, you
know. I pierced it with the hook, then folded it over and pierced
it again, then again, then again. No one . . . no one had to show
me how. I did it perfectly. *Perfectly.* All by myself."

And we leaned over and patted his knee and said, "Of course
you did, dear."

To which Chas replied, somewhat mootly: "Perfect world.
Ha!" and marched over to the barbecue pit and angrily pointed

at it, shouting, "If it's such a goddamn perfect world then you tell me for godsake why in hell I have to eat Evelyn's lousy burnt shish kebab!"

After which we, paling with horror, said absolutely nothing. Thinking instead: *Poor, poor Chas!* and then staring down at our white shoes while Chas continued to rant against life's injustices and Samuel continued to mumble about fishing and hooks and worms. . . . Staring at our shoes and finding ourselves instead confronted by the earthworm flailing against death— three inches from safety and yet it might as well have been three miles. Staring and thinking (silently, of course, secretly): *Poor Chas! Poor Samuel! What will become of them?*

And then witnessing the final spasm of that wretched worm, discerning within it a significance for which we were not exactly prepared (not quite ready—though we have had, literally, years to make ourselves ready) and so looking up, looking deeply at each other, recognizing within the dimming eyes before us the undisguised expressions of absolute (yes, we can even say *perfect)* perfect terror. Reflections of our own fear. Reflections that do not merely ask, but impolitely scream: *And what will become of us, for heaven's sake? Oh God, dear God in heaven, God of love and magic and perfection whose face we can never know . . . What will become of us all?*